Of Monsters, Men, & Moles

NATALIA LAMB

J. S. COOPER

Blurb

There was once a lamb and a big bad wolf.
He's looking for a wife and she's looking for an
adventure.
To wolf Antonio Marchesi it was all about winning.
Poor little lamb Callie Rowney didn't even realize it
was a game.

As a mafia boss, I'm meant to marry someone in my world. Someone that knows what it's like to run the world. To aid in my betrothal, my father sets up a ball and invites all the eligible women from across the country. One of them will become Mrs. Antonio Marchesi. She will be my wife. We won't be in love, but she will play her role.

Then I see the brunette in the red dress hiding in the corner of the room, trying to avoid me. She was the same woman I'd seen in the garden with her book. She's sweet, innocent, a lamb. I want her. She's totally inappropriate for the role of mafia wife. She's not from my world. Yet I can't stop my eyes from keenly following her around. And on the stroke of midnight, I make my way to talk to her, but she disappears into the night.

My roommate invited me to a party. I didn't realize it was for a mafia boss that was looking to select a wife. There were hundreds of women there, hoping to win the honor, but he's not my idea of a Prince Charming. He's tall, arrogant, cold, austere, and the most handsome man I've ever seen in my life. They call him Antonio "The Wolf" Marchesi, and the name sends a shiver down my spine. I decided to leave the party before my real identity was discovered. I climbed down a tree, slipped, and he caught me at the bottom. He held me like he didn't want to let go.

He's the head of the Marchesi Famligia: notorious, calculating, heartless. He gets everything he wants, and yet she might prove to be the one person he can't have.

Prologue

Cold air filled the room, but it didn't cool me down. My eyes searched the claustrophobic room for an exit, but I couldn't see a door. What seemed like hundreds of dark-red rose petals were scattered on the king-size bed that sat in the middle of the room. I held one of the long flowerless stems in my hand tightly, running my fingers up and down carelessly.

"Ouch," I muttered as a sharp thorn pricked my skin; I looked down to see blood running onto the viridian green stalk.

"Hurt yourself, little lamb?" The words were caring, but the voice was distinctly predatory.

"Nope," I snapped, turning to look at him with angry eyes. "Let me go."

"That didn't sound very polite." His lips twitched as he walked over to me, his tall, muscular body teasing me with its perfection. "What's the magic word?"

"Fuck off." I blinked at him, and he laughed. The distinct smell of whiskey rolled off of his tongue as he moved in closer to me, his eyes seeming darker as they came closer.

"Wrong." He grabbed my bleeding finger and held it to his eyes to observe the prick. My heart raced as his rough, warm hands covered mine. I hated that he made me feel this way. "Try again, little lamb."

"Stop calling me that. I'm not a lamb. I don't go baa."

"I know." He raised my hand to his mouth, and all air left my body as he sucked on my finger. His tongue wrapped around my skin, and his eyes never left mine as he cleaned the small cut.

"Antonio," I gasped as I attempted to push him away. My palm splayed against his crisp white shirt. I could feel his heart racing as I stared up at him. His brown eyes were like pools of passion waiting to draw me in and never let me go. I was already sinking and knew that before long I'd never be able to leave. His face was full of overgrown stubble, and his hair was unkempt. He didn't look like a man that was about to get married.

"All better now?" His tongue released my finger, and he examined it again as if he was a scientist looking through a microscope and searching for an elusive bacteria or specimen.

"Did you see the dress?" He pointed in the corner to the beautiful white, strapless gown that hung from a burnished gold rail. "It's for you." He sounded pleased as if the words should make me happy.

"Why?" I stepped away from him, my eyes surveying the room again. There had to be a door somewhere. Why couldn't I see it?

"It's a wedding gown." He grinned, a spiteful look on his face. Neither his words nor his demeanor pierced my heart. I was accustomed to his mannerisms now. I had my own steel shield locked tightly around my heart, and he would never be able to find the key.

"I can see that." I walked over to the bed and sat down. My legs were tired, and I needed some rest. That had been a mistake as he followed me over to the bed.

"Did I ever tell you the story about the wolf that became a white knight?" He brushed my curly dark hair away from my face and ran his fingers down my dirt-strewn cheek. The tip of his index finger brushed against my lips, and I opened my mouth slightly, a challenge in my eyes. He pushed his finger in slightly, and I bit down hard. He didn't even react, even though I knew it had to hurt.

"Should have been your dick," I said under my breath, and he laughed manically, his head thrown back as if I'd said the funniest comment in the world. Psycho!

"Is that your way of saying you like to suck my cock?" He nodded down, and we both saw that he was hard through his black dress pants. I would never admit it, but I felt slightly turned on as well. Why did Antonio have this effect on me?

"You wish," I spat out. I gasped suddenly as a jolt of pain shocked my brain. I closed my eyes and rubbed my forehead. I didn't feel well. The spinning of the room accompanied a black-and-white vortex, and I took a couple of deep breaths.

"Are you okay?" His tone sounded concerned, and I felt his palms brushing my hands away so that he could press his own against my forehead. "Callie, answer me."

"I'm fine." My eyes flew open, but I was lying. I felt close to throwing up. The last few months had been a whirlwind, and now here I was, feeling like I was about to die.

"Callie, mi amor..." he whispered into my ear. "Talk to me."

"I have nothing to say, Antonio." I shook my head, my voice bleak. "You should go."

"Callie..." His voice trailed off as the church bells rang out, signaling that it was noon. It was time.

"Go."

"I will come back." He kissed my lips, and I didn't stop him. Instead I reached up and grabbed his head and pulled on his silky locks. His hands ran down the side of my body, and I trembled against him. His mouth moved down to my neck, and I felt his teeth piercing my skin, sucking, making me his.

"Go." I used all my might to push him away. "You shouldn't be here."

"Callie." His voice was raspy, as his fingers gripped my face, under my neck. "I still haven't told you the fairytale I created for you. It's about a wolf and a lamb."

"I don't care." I stumbled off of the bed, anger and

tears in my eyes. "Go!" I screamed as I picked up the rose petals from the bed and threw them onto him. "Today is your wedding day, Antonio. You shouldn't be here."

"You may think I'm a monster, caro." He stepped off of the bed and shook his head. His eyes were dark and husky as he took out a pair of handcuffs and headed toward me. "But I have my reasons."

I turned my gaze to the hundreds of white candles that burned on the mantlepiece on the other side of the wall and watched as the cool breeze brought the flames alive in dance. I wouldn't listen to him anymore. I didn't understand Antonio or even myself. I had no idea how I'd gotten myself into this situation, but I was going to have to figure out a way to escape. And I knew I'd have to do it quickly.

Ring. *Ring.* The phone jolted me awake, and I blinked in the darkness. My body felt hot and sticky. My hair was slicked back against my head. I reached over to grab a glass of water and drank it down quickly.

"You okay, little lamb?" His voice sounded from behind me as he turned off the phone, and I nodded as I leaned back into his naked body. His hand crept up my stomach and cupped my breast. "Don't worry, it will be okay."

"I know," I said I as leaned down to kiss his hand and snuggle back against him. I felt his hardness pressed against my ass, and I smiled to myself, trying to ignore the feeling of unbalance in me. "Just a bad dream."

"I'll protect you." He kissed my back as his fingers rushed down and parted my legs and pushed one forward. He slipped inside of me with a single hard thrust, and I moaned as his fingers dug into my hips.

"I just can't stop thinking about—"

"Ssh!" He thrust inside of me again, slower now. "Tomorrow we will go riding...give you more pleasant thoughts."

"Okay." I closed my eyes and allowed my body to enjoy the feel of him inside of me. Antonio knew exactly what he was doing each and every time. And as he flipped me forward, I bit down into the sheets below. I knew that he'd have me screaming in ecstasy in a few seconds, and I didn't want Jimmy rushing into the bedroom again. He'd already seen far too much the first time.

CHAPTER 1

Antonio

"Revenge is an act of passion; vengeance of justice. Injuries are revenged; crimes are avenged." Samuel Johnson

I was going to be a husband.

The thought was unpleasant to my brain. Men like me didn't become husbands. It wasn't a relationship I was looking forward to, but I knew I had no say in my future.

I tapped my foot in beat to the ticking sound emanating from the radiator as my father talked. We needed to get the heater fixed. I could smell the warm must of mildew circling the dark room as three men sat at the back table counting several hundred stacks of cash.

The clanking sounds of pots and pans filled the

room. Our makeshift warehouse sat next to the kitchen, but unless you knew where the secret door was, you'd have no clue. The restaurant was busy today, and there was a line halfway up the street, thanks to the many tourists that had seen a few TikTok videos stating we had the most authentic pasta in the city. If the crowds continued, we'd have to find another place to count the cash.

"Antonio, are you listening to me?" My father's raspy voice sounded irritated as he held his stubby fingers up in the air.

"When do I not?" I said, an edge to my voice that even I could hear. My father annoyed me on the best of days, but today, today I wanted to staple his lips together to stop him from talking.

"There will be a ball with hundreds of women attending. Families from New York, Chicago, Sicil-ia." My father's voice paused as his steely blue eyes sized me up. "You will choose a wife." He walked over to me, gripping my shoulder tightly as he squeezed. "You will marry, and you know why?"

"Why?" I wanted to punch his face in. We both knew why.

"Because your don says so." He smirked. My father, Don Roberto Marchesi, was the leader of the largest mafia family in New York. He wielded power that was unheard of since the 1980s, and he never missed an opportunity to remind me of that fact. He commanded the respect of thousands of men, and even though I was his underboss, I was still powerless without him. But one day, one day, it would all be mine.

"Yes, Papa." I nodded my agreement at him. "You're lucky you caught me on a good day."

"What did you fucking say?" He was pissed at my insolence. His dark eyes bore into mine for a few moments before he took a step toward me. "I'll fucking—"

"You'll do what?" I grabbed his wrist and held it up, using only a tenth of my strength against him. "You'll do shit." He knew better than to piss me off.

"Hey, Roberto." Tommasso, his consigliere, stepped forward from the shadows. "The boys see some markings on the twenties. We need to disperse them." He stood there in his navy-blue, pinstriped suit looking like a Wall Street prick, his hair smoothed back with so much gel that a kid could slide back and forth like a Slip-n-Slide.

"Where'd they come from?" My dad lightly rubbed his right eyebrow. Whoever sent the dirty cash would be lucky to escape the week with their life.

"Mambo's Pizzeria in Prospect Park," Tommasso responded. "I warned you about Jimmy and his guys."

"Deal with it."

"Yes, boss." Tommasso nodded his head imperceptibly, a smirk on his face as he retreated back toward the table.

"I don't care if you want this marriage or not, Antonio," he spat out as if he weren't just interrupted. "I don't care if you're happy, if you fuck her once a year or every night like a fucking bunny rabbit. Fuck, I don't even care if she fucks you up the ass because that's what you want, but the one thing I know is that you will marry." My father was the only one allowed to talk to me in that way and keep his life. He was my father and the leader of our family—for now. I wondered which families would eagerly send their daughters to wed me. I'd made a name for myself in New York, Philly, Chicago, Boston, and Detroit. Antonio "The Wolf" Marchesi was what they called me. I was known for breaking hearts, arms, and being above the law. There were many members of the mafia—cosa nostra, as we called it—that would like to make a match. I'd even fucked a few of them already.

"She must be from one of the top families…" He was still talking, but I wasn't listening. His voice was floating in the air like music notes to a song I didn't know. My tongue flicked around my mouth as I stood there. There was still grit in my teeth from the momentary brush my face made with the ground earlier in the day at the boxing ring. My stomach burned from consuming too much cheap whiskey after the fight. Jimmy never bought the good stuff. Fucking idiot. He liked to live like a pauper for no reason. But that's why I trusted him. He wasn't in the game for wealth. He was in it for duty.

Father was going on and on about the need to protect the Marchesi name. He talked about his grandfather and his father before him and how the name stood for something. He acted like we're angels of the earth, protecting everyone that surrounded us, and I wanted to laugh, but I knew better than that. My father didn't like the sound of laughter. He saw it as a slight. Many a man had lost his head over impromptu laughter. Suddenly, I noticed silence had filled the air. Fuck, I'd chuckled without realizing it.

"You think this is funny?" he said, pulling his gun and shooting a target above my head. I didn't flinch.

"What I think is funny is that you're taking this so seriously. Like you were ever a good husband. Not to Mom and not to any of your other wives." My eyes met his, cold versus cold, and hatred bubbled around us like a cloud.

He paused for a few moments, and I watched as he looked back across the room to make sure everything was as it should be. The evil smile on his pudgy face was a sight to see as he nodded his pleasure at what he saw.

"That fucking mouth of yours will get you in trouble when you're don." He blew a kiss toward the back of the room. "Nearly done, Bambi, then I'm all yours."

The blonde, whom my stepmother knew nothing about, was on her knees waiting to finish her job successfully. He'd blow his load, either in her mouth or on her face, and then dismiss her. She'd walk out with her head high, proud she'd made him come, thinking she's special. But she's just another whore in a long line of whores that meant nothing to him.

The men were still counting the cash that came in this morning. I'd estimate a cool half-mill by the time it's taking them to count. This made my father happier than the blonde, not that she realized that. Nothing meant anything to Don Roberto but the famiglia. And the actual people in the famiglia came second to the power and money. Those were the only two things that turned my father on. And that's how I knew I'd make a better leader than him. Because nothing in my life revolved around power or money. My world's axis was held up by revenge.

My mind drifted off, thinking about the redhead in the coffee shop from earlier in the day. She'd taken ten minutes to decide what drink she wanted and did not have enough money to pay. So I'd stepped in, put it on my card. She blushed and thanked me furiously. I'd shrugged, just wanting her to hurry up. Jimmy, being the asshole that he was, had told her to blow me if she was that grateful, and she'd gone even redder. I'd laughed because she'd had a pretty face but wasn't my type. She wasn't the sort of girl mafioso men messed with: too timid. I liked my women loud, feisty, and sexy as sin. Women that messed with me knew they were getting one thing and one thing only: the orgasm of their lives. Nothing was better than hearing a woman scream out my name in the throes of ecstasy.

"Antonio, do you hear what I'm saying?" My father's raspy voice was close to my face; I could smell the smoke from his cigarette in my nostrils. I nodded. I was being dismissed. "You don't have to love her, but you still have to choose."

"I will, Papa." I took a step back. I would choose a wife, but not because I wanted to. It was my duty. I was never going to fall for anyone. That's not what Marchesi men did. Maybe I wouldn't even get married. That would shock him.

My phone beeped then, and I pulled it out of my pocket. I swiped on the message from Jimmy and chuckled. It was a photo of him and the redhead in bed, naked. I didn't even know they'd exchanged numbers, but Jimmy certainly always got what he wanted.

"This is not how we do things normally." I heard the clicking of the trigger again, and I looked up. My father's pointing it above my head again. "You paying attention to me, Antonio?"

"I'm listening." My heart didn't even skip a beat as I stepped forward, twisted his arm, and released the gun from his grasp. He didn't get to play games with me twice in one day. I pushed the gun against his head and saw his pale face trembling. "Don't fuck with me, Papa." I saw two of his soldiers stepping forward, arms cocked and ready for a blood fight, but I didn't care.

"Drop the gun." Papa's voice was steely. He knew I wouldn't pull the trigger. He's more embarrassed being shown up in front of his men, by his second in command, but I didn't give a shit. His time had nearly come, and he didn't even know it.

"Who's in trouble?" The easygoing voice of my younger brother, Alessandro, entered the room. He's dressed all in black, with his shirt unbuttoned, exposing a thick patch of hair. He looked the blonde up and down, licked his lips, and headed over to me. "Antonio, what have you done to Daddy Dearest to make him so pissed?"

My father snorted while Alessandro pushed my hand away from his head. Alessandro liked to keep the peace. "And Papa, what have you done to Antonio to make him such a hothead?" He laughed.

Alessandro gave me a quick hug, and I pushed him away as his eyes surveyed mine. My father looked at him in disgust. Alessandro was a disappointment to him with his constant jokes and lothario ways. He also hated how loyal he was to me. My father wanted to pit us against each other, but he failed.

"We're just discussing my wedding and how my dick will only be in one fucking pussy for the rest of its life." I shook my head in disgust. "What are you doing?"

"We have a problem in the Bronx." He shrugged. "Giovanni said they think they have some under-covers in one of the dens playing poker."

"He can't take care of it?" Giovanni was one of the made men in the organization. He made sure our illegal gambling businesses ran smoothly, and when they didn't, he took care of it. He helped to enforce the rules. He wasn't the only made man in the family, but he was the most respected.

"He can." Alessandro gave me a look. This was his way of giving me an out with Papa, and I'd nearly fucked it up.

"Fine. Let's head to the Bronx." I looked over at my dad. "Just tell me the time and date of the ball, and I'll be there." I grabbed my holster and slipped it around my waist as I walked to the door. "Come on." I looked back at Alessandro. "Let's go put out some fires." My brother followed behind me, saluting our dad as we left the room and through the busy kitchen. Head Chef Mario saluted us right before bringing his butcher knife down to cut off a pig's tongue.

"Let's head to Florence on Fifth," he said with a wide smile, and I gave him a questioning look. He held up his pinky finger and rubbed the family insignia softly. I had a similar ring. We'd had that made when we were older. They were a remembrance of our mother and close to our hearts. I knew exactly what he was saying.

"Let's go." I smiled at him as we headed out the back door to the alleyway. Frankie, my driver, was waiting with a black Sports Range Rover, and we jumped into the backseat. I was going to be a husband. This was the moment I'd been waiting for all my life.

CHAPTER 2

Callie

"Rare as is true love, true friendship is rarer." Jean de La Fontaine

I was never getting married.

Not because I didn't want to, but because my love life absolutely sucked. If there was an award for nonexistent soulmate, I would win. Dinosaurs would be back on earth before I got married. That's the rate in which men were flocking to be by my side.

10:30 p.m. The number flashed on my phone as I stretched out on my twin-size bed. The sound of Harry Styles' voice echoed in the room through my small orange Bose speaker. I debated between grabbing my laptop to watch the latest season of *You*—I loved Penn Badgley—or reading a book.

I knew I should probably go to sleep, but it was a Saturday night, and I didn't want to feel like a complete loser. Sometimes I wondered when my life would actually start. Between my college classes, job, books, and hanging out with friends, I didn't seem to have time for an adventure. And I craved an adventure in my life. Particularly a romantic one. Though I'd have to change out of my Snoopy PJs before I embarked on a whirlwind romance with some hot man that couldn't resist me.

I had a recurring dream about once a week. I was in a long corridor, holding a dark bronze candelabra with three tall, slim, white candles. At the end of the corridor were five doors, and I had to choose one to go into. I was told that behind each door was one man that could be the love of my life. Every time I was about to make a decision and walk to a door to meet my soulmate, I woke up. Even in my dreams, my life was a mystery.

I had no idea what it meant to keep having the same dream over and over again. I supposed it's just my anxiety playing out through my dreams. I was a college senior, about to graduate in five months, and I had no idea what I wanted to do with my life. There was the princess fantasy where I dreamed of getting whisked away to some foreign land where I played with children in the street and baked cookies for senior citizens, but I didn't think that's happening anytime soon.

I'd thought about applying to grad schools as the logical next step. I was getting my bachelor's degree in psychology, and all of my professors had told me that if I even wanted to think about being a psychologist, I had to continue my education. I was not sure how I felt about that. Seventy-five thousand dollars in student loan debt already felt like quite a lot, and I was not sure I actually wanted to be a psychologist. I'd found that people were far too messed up, even for me, thus my hesitation. There were so many different options in life, and yet none of them seemed very appealing.

"Callie, are you coming out tonight?" my roommate Valentina asked me, though I knew she didn't care if I chose to go or stay. She was the complete opposite of me, with her perfectly straight raven hair and exotic purple-blue eyes. Tonight she'd highlighted her eyes with a gold eyeshadow to match her sparkly top. She's as glamorous as a high-fashion model, and I bought my clothes at Target and barely wore makeup. We'd been roommates for two years now, and I still felt like I was trying to figure her out. I would say that we were friends, but she didn't even know my last name.

"I don't think so." I shook my head and leaned back against the wall. My legs were crossed in front of me, and I had a puzzle book on the mattress, open to page twenty-five of eighty. I played with the black pen in my hand as I stared at the number puzzle.

Was I a lame brain for staying home almost every weekend reading and studying?

"How are you ever going to get laid if all you do is draw?" Valentina sprayed herself with the Vera Wang perfume my father had gifted me for my birthday and fluffed her hair.

"I'm not drawing." I held up the puzzle book. "I'm doing a Sudoku—"

"I know you're an art major, but there's more to life than painting." Valentina opened my closet and pulled out my adored vintage Chanel handbag. "I'm borrowing this," she said as she twirled around, grasping it to her side.

"No…" I protested weakly as my heart sank. It had been my late mother's, and it was my prized possession.

"Ciao." She grabbed her phone and left the room without even looking at me. "Maksim, I'm headed downstairs." She spoke into the phone in an irritated voice.

"Goodbye, Valentina," I said as she slammed the door behind her. "I'm a psychology major, and I can't paint or draw anything to save my life." I sighed as I got up off of the bed and walked to my closet door and closed it. I said a little prayer that my beloved handbag would survive the night. I needed to grow a backbone.

I walked to the other side of the room and stared at my reflection in the mirror. "You need a makeover, Callie Rowney, but with all the sex you're not having, I'm not sure it matters." My mouth twisted at my self-deprecating joke. I didn't want to be a virgin. I was still waiting for my first sexual adventure, but all the men I met in college were dorks or jocks that wouldn't understand the rules of romance if they were handed to them on a silver platter.

I reached for my romance book and plumped up one of my down feather pillows before settling back down. I grabbed my phone and turned off the music to concentrate on my book. As I went to open the pages, it suddenly struck me that here I was, reading about love, and there Valentina was experiencing it. And if her words were to be believed, she was experiencing it with a different man every month. I couldn't even imagine dating and sleeping with that many men. Though a part of me wished I could experience what it would be like to be desired by so many men. Her latest guy, Maksim, was dark, tattooed, and hot. He reminded me of a modern-day Dracula. He had this brooding intensity that scared and intrigued me at the same time. I'd only met him once, though, so I wasn't sure of his personality.

I sighed, suddenly feeling sorry for myself, and decided to call my best friend Imogen instead. Imogen lived in California now, so I knew she had to be awake still. The phone rang two times, and then she answered breathlessly.

"Callie, what are you up to?" she said and then started coughing.

"Are you okay?" I asked, worried she would have a coughing fit and die with me on the phone.

"Yes, sorry. I went for a run, but I forgot I hate running and that I'm out of shape." She half giggled and then started coughing again. "Remind me to never try getting into shape again."

"I will," I said and smiled as I thought about all the times we'd both attempted to lose weight and get fit. We'd spent our entire teen years talking about how much better our lives would be if we were just size zeroes.

"What are you doing up so late?" she asked, and I had to admit that her question made me feel like a loser. Certainly no glamour girls were expected to be in bed before midnight on a Friday night. I was a college senior, for heaven's sake. I should be out partying, having the time of my life.

"Couldn't sleep. I'm thinking of watching a movie."

"Ooh, you should finally watch *The Godfather*. I can't believe you've never seen it."

"I'm not interested in mafia movies." I wrinkled my nose as I thought about all the violence such a movie would hold. "I was thinking *Fifty First Dates*."

"You've seen that so many times, Callie," she reminded me as if I could have forgotten. I'd seen the romantic comedy with her at least ten times. It was my favorite movie. I loved Adam Sandler and Drew Barrymore, and I loved how patient he was with her.

"Maybe I'll watch *The Talented Mr. Ripley* with Matt Damon instead. I've heard that's good."

"If you're into movies about men who lie to get ahead." She laughed. "Oh, wait, that's all men."

"Still going through a bad time with Joshua?" Joshua was her on-again off-again friend with benefits that had gotten complicated. She wanted more, and while he continued to string her along, it was obvious to everyone but her that all he wanted was sex.

"I'm done with him," she said, her voice adamant. I would have believed her if she hadn't said the same thing many times before.

"I'm sorry. I wish I was there to buy you ice cream."

"They don't eat real ice cream in Berkeley," she scoffed. "I wish I was back in New York with you."

"You'll be back soon, right? You're coming home for Thanksgiving?"

"Yeah, your dad invited my dad and me, remember? My mom will be in Florence with her art group."

"That will be fun," I said wistfully. Imogen's mom had quit her job as a banker at fifty to pursue her love of sculpture. She wasn't very talented, but she was certainly giving it her all. Imogen's dad worked for the mayor and didn't seem to mind that his wife was traveling around the world every couple of weeks. Sometimes I wished I could just pack up and travel. My life was so boring. I just wanted an adventure.

"Callie, can I call you tomorrow? Josh just texted, and he wants to study in the library."

"Uh huh," I said, not wanting to be the friend that said, "Why are you giving it up so easily for a man that doesn't value you?"

"Have a great evening," she said breathlessly, and I knew she had run to the bathroom to reapply her makeup and push up her bra.

"Night, Imogen. Have fun." I hung up the phone, and a wave of sorrow washed over me. I was twenty-one years old, and my life felt mundane and boring. I'd never had a great romantic affair, I'd never gone to a raving all-night party, and I'd never had sex; I'd essentially never lived. I stared at my unpainted fingernails and unadorned fingers and wrists. I didn't even have any jewelry. No man had ever bought me flowers, besides my dad. And he was a bit of a sad case. I loved him, but he had never gotten over my mom's death when I was two. He'd remained celibate for all these years because he'd loved her so much. I longed for someone to love me as much as my father had loved my mother. Someone that would think the world began and ended with me. Someone who wouldn't even think of looking at another woman.

"That's enough, Callie," I lectured myself as I jumped off of the bed and grabbed my toothbrush. I would go to the shared bathrooms every undergrad used on the floor, brush my teeth, and then try and watch a movie. And maybe if I was lucky I'd have dreams about meeting the love of my life. It never hurt to dream. It was just sad that my dreams were better than my reality.

CHAPTER 3

Antonio

"Life being what it is, one dreams of revenge." — *Paul Gauguin*

Florence on Fifth was our most popular bar and was constantly packed with people. There were five levels featuring different styles of music and drinks, and we were listed in every "Where to Go in New York" article written in the last ten years.

"Antonio, Alessandro." The beefy bodyguard nodded at us as we walked past the long line of customers waiting to get in. "I didn't know yous two were going to be here tonight."

"Just dropping in." I looked over at the four women standing at the front of the line, each more scantily clad than the other. "We're just checking out the scenery."

"Yes, boss." He smacked his lips as he checked out the beautiful women and held up the deep red velvet rope and let us in. "Have a good night."

"We will, Mikey." I waited for Alessandro to join me as he was already engaged in a flirtatious conversation with a redhead in the line. What was with it with redheads today?

"Come on," I snapped at my brother as he pulled out his phone to get a number. "We have work to do."

"You're all work and no play. You have to lighten up, Antonio."

"There is no such thing as lighten up." I frowned at my brother and his boyish grin. To any innocent passerby seeing him, they would think he was a handsome, slightly flirtatious, overeager lothario that couldn't hurt a fly. I knew better than that. My brother was, after all, a Marchesi. Some may say he had an even better shot than me. And when it came to business, he could be even more intense. Many in the family even worried he would try and usurp me one day, when I became don, but I knew better. Alessandro didn't want ultimate control and power, as I did. We were only two years apart in age, but we couldn't be more different. His want didn't influence his life goals to be a leader.

"Well, hello there, big boy." A familiar pretty woman with a short fro started dancing in front of me.

"Hello to you, too." I nodded and smiled slightly as she gave me the eye. I could see security guards all around the periphery of the bar eyeing the situation. My soldiers were always at the ready. I looked over at Vinny and shook my head. Everything was good here. "How are you doing, Tanya?" I kissed her on both cheeks.

"Just here hoping to see you." She hooked her arm through mine. "Buy me a drink."

"I'm here for business tonight, not pleasure." I shook my head regretfully. "But tell the bartender, Joey, it's on me."

"Antonio." She pouted. "You won't have a drink with me?"

"Maybe later."

"I'll have one with you, beautiful." Alessandro stepped forward, and she laughed happily. Tanya loved my brother even more than me.

"I didn't see you there." Her glowing dark eyes were vibrant as she stared at us. "When are you boys going to join me on a trip to Ghana? You will have so much fun."

"One day." I smiled. Tanya's father was a prominent businessman in Ghana, and he had provided furnishings for several of my businesses at discount prices. In exchange, I always ensured to hook up him and his friends with whatever they needed Stateside. Everything wasn't always above board, but nothing in life ever really was.

"I'll hold you to that, Marchesi." She touched her fingers to the gold necklace around her throat and rubbed the pearl before letting her fingers drift down toward the valley between her breasts. My eyes followed the movement of her fingers, and she giggled slightly. Tanya was gorgeous. And I knew she'd be terrific in bed, but I didn't fancy getting on her father's bad side. No father was pleased to hear their daughter was messing around with Antonio Marchesi. I was the last man in the world men wanted their princesses to be with. I was a father's nightmare. If I wanted to get revenge on someone, I'd date their daughter. That would make them burn. I laughed to myself at the thought. If Tanya's dad could see his innocent, sweet daughter right now, he'd send her back to Ghana before she could say limoncello.

"You have a nice night, doll." I gave her a nod. "Any word?" I looked back at Alessandro, and he nodded, his face taut as he held up his phone. He must have gotten a text.

"Upstairs." He pointed toward the elevator. "In the high-stakes poker room."

"Perfect." I made my way through the crowds of people toward the VIP elevator at the back of the room. Bodies were gyrating in beat to the House music blasting through the speakers. Sexy women in skimpy costumes walked through the club with trays of overpriced cocktail shots for the patrons to buy. I had four men walking around, making sure no drugs were being sold outside of Vinny's stash. He sold clean. Nothing was mixed. No fentanyl overdoses were going to happen at any of my places. In fact, the Marchesi famiglia no longer dealt with drugs. We'd had a cocaine stint in the eighties and nineties that had made us a lot of money, but drugs made you too high profile. And brought you had karma. Many of the top families had ruined entire communities with their introduction of heroine. Yeah, it had been big money, but karma was a bitch. The best move my father had ever made for the family, maybe the only good move, was legitimizing our businesses as much as possible. We weren't one hundred percent legit, of course. But at least innocent kids experimenting with drugs for the first time weren't dying because of us.

Alessandro and I walked into the elevator, and as the doors closed, he took a small silver container out of his pocket and offered it to me. "Bump?"

"No."

He shrugged and tapped his fingers against the top of the metal. The sound was irritating, but I didn't say anything. He knew he was annoying me.

"You don't have to get married if you really don't want to." The finger tapping was getting louder now. "Just tell Papa to stick it where the sun don't shine and he'll back off."

"We have to have the ball. The invitations have been sent out."

"Like you care." He frowned. "Oh yeah, I forgot to tell you. The Romanos want us to go over for dinner tomorrow night. Papa has already said yes. You know Tommasso wants you to marry Angelica."

"I know he does, and it's not going to happen."

"You going to tell him she bats for her own team?" Alessandro snorted, and I shook my head. There were many things I wasn't going to tell Tommasso, including the fact that I'd slept with his other daughter Serena a couple of years ago and that she'd been a fucking nightmare to get rid of. Must have been that good Marchesi dick.

The elevator doors beeped, and we made our way down the dark hallway to the select players club. We walked side by side in the darkness, the music and laughter coming from the room drawing us in.

"Let me handle this." I stopped before we walked into the door.

"Of course. You are the chosen one, after all."

"I didn't ask for this, Alessandro."

"I know." He squeezed my shoulder. "Not having second thoughts, are you?"

"Of course not." My voice was cold. "I've been waiting a long time for this day."

"Then let us proceed." Alessandro's voice was low. "For Mom's memory."

"For Mom." I nodded and pushed the door open.

The room was packed; stacks of chips sat on the tables, and drunk mobsters, politicians, business-men, and celebrities sat around gambling, hoping not to lose everything. My eyes surveyed the room three times before I spied the prize I was seeking.

"Vee." I leaned down and kissed both cheeks. "How are you?"

"Bored." She yawned, her eyes looking dull. She was coked up. "You?"

"The same." I sat down in the empty seat next to her. I could see her boyfriend eyeing me up from the other side. I could tell he was jealous, but he knew not to say anything to me. "I have a favor to ask you."

"Oh?" She raised an eyebrow, her attention now fully on me. "Another?"

"I have a proposition for you." I smiled at her languidly and leaned back. "Business related. You'll be well compensated."

"Is this going to get me in trouble with the law?" she asked innocently, her eyes thinking up big numbers for the risk.

"Is that really a question you're going to ask me here?" I looked around the room. There were two state senators, one governor (on his way out, but he didn't know it), two high-ranking cops, and the Mayor of New York. My eyes focused on him. I had plans for him. Big plans, but I had to take one thing at a time. In politics, you couldn't play your cards unless you were one hundred percent sure you had the winning hand.

"Fine." She rolled her eyes. "I'm listening." And just like that, the first puzzle piece was on the way to fitting in. It was funny how life worked. You could go your whole life waiting for something to happen. It could take so long that it seemed like it would never be possible. But then one thing changed, and all of your dreams felt like they had a real possibility of coming true. Some people said that a life of crime didn't pay, and I said that nothing paid unless you're willing to get your hands dirty in some way.

CHAPTER 4

Callie

"True love is selfless. It is prepared to sacrifice." —Sadhu Vaswani

"Hey, Callie, how's it going?" Valentina walked toward me, a playful expression on her face. I looked at her in surprise, every instinct in my body telling me something was up. She never spoke pleasantly, and I wasn't used to it. I hadn't seen her in a few days, though, so maybe she'd missed me. Though I doubted it.

"Hey, what's up?" I asked her, folding my book and placing it beside me on the mattress.

"You love to read, don't you?" Her long, dark hair swayed back and forth as she sashayed over to me. The gold bangles on her wrists made a light clanking sound as her arms swung back and forth, and I admired how trendy she always looked.

"Yeah, I do." I nodded. I wondered if she was going to ask me for some book recommendations, and I knew I could spend the next hour talking about my favorite three books.

"What are you reading?" she asked, sitting down on my bed next to me. I glanced into her blue eyes and noticed that she genuinely looked interested, which surprised me. Valentina didn't care about anything I read. I'd never even seen her studying. I was shocked that she was still enrolled in school as a student as I had no idea how she was passing any of her classes. Maybe she was sleeping with her professors to get passing grades. I'd heard rumors that some of the girls in the English department did that, but I had no clue if it was true.

"Oh, it's this really cool speculative fiction book called *Babel*. It's written by—"

"Oh, cool. Cool." Valentina nodded, cutting me off. She tapped her fingers against her leg and then offered me the warmest smile she'd ever given me. And I'd lived with her for two years now. "So what are you up to tonight?"

"Reading." I held up the book to her again. "Why?"

"I was wondering if you wanted to go to a party," she asked, sounding excited. Her blue eyes gazed into mine, and I could sense a pleading in her tone. "I mean, if you want to."

"I don't know," I said, shaking my head. I wasn't really much into parties where I didn't know the people.

"It'll be fun, I promise." She gave me a dazzling smile, like she really wanted me to go.

"Okay," I said, laughing. "My friend Rachel and I were meant to go to a comedy show tonight, but she canceled on me because she met—"

"Oh, comedy shows are so mundane. They're so 2010," she said, and I bit down on my lower lip.

"Well, the party sounds fun. What time are we going?"

"Well, about that," she said, wrinkling her nose. "*We're* not going."

"What do you mean we're not going? You just asked me if I wanted to go." I played with my long, black hair and frowned. She was confusing me.

"No, I mean, you are going, but I won't be able to make it."

"Oh, I don't feel comfortable going to a party alone. I don't even know the people throwing the party." What a weird invitation. I mean, I was shocked she'd offered me an invitation in the first place, but this was even more unbelievable.

"It'll be fine. I have everything set up for you already," she said, jumping up. She hurried over to her side of the bedroom and opened her closet. She picked up a red dress and handed it to me. "You'll wear this."

"Huh?" I said, staring at the glamorous silk dress. "What'd you mean?"

"I got this to wear tonight, but you can wear it instead."

"To a party?" I frowned. What sort of party was this? The afterparty of the Met Gala or something?

"And another thing, Callie..." She gave me her most winning smile, and I could feel my heart racing. Why was she being so nice to me? Valentina was never nice to me.

"Yeah?" I said timidly, not really sure I wanted to know what she was going to say next.

"Well, you'll have to pretend you're me to get in."

"Oh, no." I shook my head vehemently. "I don't think so. I'm not really a liar, and I don't really want to go to this party."

"Please." She dropped to her knees in front of me, and my jaw dropped. There were tears in her eyes, and my heart started thudding. What was going on here? I'd never seen Valentina look distraught. "I don't want to go to this party. My dad wants me to go because it's a family friend, but I really want to see my boyfriend, Maksim. My dad disapproves of him. I'm like the modern-day Juliet right now, and it's not like anyone at the party knows me. So if you just went and pretended to be me, it would mean the world." She clutched her heart, and my jaw dropped.

I'd had no idea she was in a forbidden relationship. "You will have lots of free drinks and meet some cool people that might make you want to start getting out of this room more often." She wiped her tears away and looked at me pointedly. She had a point, but ouch, her comment hurt.

I sighed. "Well, I enjoy reading, and I was thinking of signing up for an acre yoga class."

"I hear you on the phone almost every week talking to your friends, complaining that you have no life, nothing ever happens, and you want an adventure. Don't you want to meet a really good-looking guy? Well, tonight's the night, Callie. Tonight, I promise there will be many good-looking men all dressed in suits, all looking at you and thinking, *Wow, she's gorgeous.*"

I stared at her in disbelief, and she sighed as she glanced at my attire. "Okay. I mean, you don't look gorgeous right now. You're kind of an ugly duckling. It doesn't look like you've waxed your eyebrows in years or ever threaded your upper lip, and while I've never seen you put on a full face of makeup or flat-iron your hair, you're cute." I thought she realized that her comments were underwhelming because she added, "I think with my help, you can look pretty darn good. Really pretty."

I swallowed hard. I didn't really know what to say to that. She'd completely dissed my appearance. I mean, she was right. I'd only gotten my eyebrows waxed once in my life, and they'd hurt like shit, so I never went back. I never threaded my upper lip because I'd been using a bleach cream, which obviously was not working, and I tried with makeup; I just didn't really know how to apply it. I stared at her. "I don't know, Valentina. I just don't feel comfortable going to—"

"Please. It will just be for a little bit. You can go for an hour and then leave. Just so they know you were there." She giggled. "Well, I mean, I was there. Please. My boyfriend said he'll dump me if I don't go to this thing with him tonight, and well, he's the love of my life, and I know that you understand what it is to have met the love of your life. You'll do any and everything for them." I stared at her, not really knowing what to say. I'd never met the love of my life. I'd never had a love, but she knew I read a lot, and she knew I loved romance. I watched romcoms almost every week. I had a stack of about twenty romance books next to my bed, and I talked with my friends about romance on a nightly basis on the phone.

"Fine," I said, "I'll go, but only for an hour."

"Thank you so much." She jumped up and hugged me. She smelled like roses. The smell was sweet at first but immediately started to feel pungent and overwhelming. She had far too much of it on.

"That's a really nice perfume," I said softly, trying not to cover my nose.

"You can borrow it," she said, rushing over to her side of the room, picking up a small pink glass bottle. "Actually, you can have it."

"Oh no, that's okay." I really didn't want it.

"No, it's on me," she said. "My dad's rich. He can buy me ten more."

"Well, thank you," I said. That was something I knew to be true. Valentina's dad, though I'd never met him, was loaded. He sent limos for her to go out like every single day, which I thought was absolutely ridiculous. Never before in my life had I ever seen anyone getting in a limo aside from prom and homecoming. Not only did he send limos, but he also had a driver for her and two bodyguards. She had never told me what he did for a living, but I'd assumed that he was a diplomat for some small, exotic island nation somewhere, most probably one I'd never heard of before. She never spoke about him, so I assumed that she was trying to keep her actual identity on the down low. I figured if my dad was a president or a diplomat of a country, I would want to do the same.

"So wear this dress," she said, dropping it on my bed. Her tone was dismissive. "And I have a little tiara for you to wear."

"A tiara?" I raised an eyebrow. "What sort of party is this exactly?"

"Oh, it's just a little ball. Like a fancy dress party."

"A fancy dress party?"

"Look, here's a gold mask. You can wear this, too."

"Okay. Is this stuff mandatory or..." She stared at me for a couple of seconds, and I thought she could sense my hesitancy because she shook her head quickly.

"Not at all. If you one hundred percent don't feel confident wearing it, you can wear whatever you want to wear, but still let me do your makeup and stuff, okay?"

"Okay." I nodded, staring at the dress.

"Oh, and here are some heels you can wear." She pointed to the black, slinky stilettos that she'd worn the night before that were still sitting next to our door. "Okay, go and have a shower. Shave all your bits," she said, laughing in a not-very-kind way.

"Sorry? What do you mean, shave all my bits?"

"Well, your legs, under your arms. Your arms, because they're kind of hairy."

"Shave my arms?"

"Yeah, girl. And maybe your pubes."

"What? Why would I do that?"

"Who knows? Maybe you'll get lucky tonight."

"I don't even know anyone at the party, Valentina. I'm not going to have sex."

"Oh, yeah." She burst out laughing. "I forgot. You're a *virgin*, aren't you?"

I nodded slowly, not liking the way she'd said the word, as if it was something really bad. I mean, I knew that it made me different to most of the women at our university because pretty much everyone had hooked up with someone, but I liked to think it made me special. Not better than anyone else, because if I could have got laid, I would have. At least if it was with someone really hot that I really liked, not just some random guy from philosophy class that had acne all over his face and still had braces and said he'd do me for $20, like Thomas Sewell Scott had done the year before, but that was another story. He was absolutely gross. I wanted a man for my first time. I'd shave every hair on my body for one night with a sexy Henry Cavill lookalike.

"Hey, Callie." Valentina snapped her fingers in front of my face.

"Yeah?" I asked her, blinking.

"Shower. Now. I have to leave here in an hour to meet my boyfriend, and you have to get to the party within an hour and forty-five minutes."

"Where is the party exactly?" I asked her, frowning.

"Don't worry about it. A limo will pick you up and take you, and it will bring you back as well."

"Oh, you don't have to do that. I can catch an Uber or something."

She shook her head. "No, Ubers won't be allowed into the place you're going."

"Huh?" I asked her. "What do you mean? Isn't it in the city? Where in Manhattan can Ubers not go?"

"No," she said, shaking her head. "It's not in the city."

"Oh, where is it?"

"Don't worry about it," she said. "The limo will take you."

"Okay." I knew that it wasn't smart of me to get into a limo and go to an unknown destination without telling anyone or having any sort of information. My father had always told me if I was going somewhere, make sure I knew the address so that if I had to call the police, they knew where to pick me up. But Valentina was my roommate. She wasn't exactly my friend, but we lived together for years. She was someone that I could trust. She wouldn't let anything bad happen to me.

"It will be an adventure, Callie. Haven't you always wanted an adventure? Let your love life start tonight."

"I don't know about all that, but fine," I said, jumping up. "I'm going to go in the shower now."

"Good, and don't forget—"

"I know. I'll shave as much as I can," I said, biting down on my lower lip to stop from making a snide remark.

"Hey, wait up," she said, opening the drawer next to her bed.

"Oh. What is it?" I asked her as she handed me a pink-and-purple bottle.

"Hair removing cream," she said, shaking her head.

"Oh. Why are you giving me this?"

"It's a bikini wax removing cream. It's not exactly a wax. It's just a depilatory. But if you haven't ever shaved down there, it could take a while, so use this. It'll be faster."

"Oh, thank you." I felt embarrassed and could feel my face going red at her comments. It was true, of course. I'd never shaved down there or waxed down there. I hadn't had a reason. I sighed as I made my way through the door toward the bathroom. I could hear two of the guys who lived two rooms down laughing about something as they made their way out the corridor.

"Hey there, Callie," Josh said, his green eyes laughing as he stared at me. He stopped and leaned against the way. "I'll see you in the room, Mike," he commented to his friend, who had continued walking.

"I'll turn on the PS5," Mike said as he hurried to their shared dorm.

"Hey, Josh. How's it going?" I asked him, feeling slightly embarrassed after our last get-together.

"Not bad." Josh was on the baseball team, one of the better-looking and nicer guys that lived on the same floor as me. He was a total player, though.

Every weekend I saw a different girl going into his room. Which made our experience stand out to me, even more.

"What are you up to tonight?" he said. "You want to hang out?"

"No," I said quickly. "Thanks, though."

"Pity," he said. He looked slightly disappointed, which surprised me because Josh could have and did have any woman he wanted. "Well, let me know if you change your mind," he said eagerly. I wondered if he wanted a second chance to be intimate with me. Josh and I had gone on two quasi dates. The last one had ended up in his room, and I'd been quite excited as I thought he was really attractive. We'd both been drunk, and we'd made out a little bit. He'd attempted to pull my panties off, telling me how much he was going to make me come. His words had sounded eager and a bit crass, but I'd been down for it. But then he'd passed out, my panties halfway down my legs. I wasn't sure who'd been more embarrassed when I'd finally nudged him awake so I could leave and go back to my own dorm. I hadn't told anyone about that night. And it made me feel quite self-conscious.

"Oh, I'm actually going to a party tonight."

He looked shocked as he ran his fingers through his dirty blond hair. "No way. What party?"

"Oh, a ball," I said, grinning, trying to fake that I was super excited. "Not a college thing."

"A ball?" He raised an eyebrow. I could tell he was even more shocked. I was not the sort of girl that went to balls.

"Yeah, Valentina invited me." Which was true. I wasn't going to tell him that I was going pretending I was Valentina or that the whole thing sounded slightly off. I didn't want to think about how sketchy the situation seemed, because it did seem sketchy. Why couldn't Valentina just tell her parents she didn't want to go, and why couldn't she just skip it, and why weren't her parents going if it was so important? I had so many questions that I knew I would never get answers to, but she was right. It would be an adventure. It would be something different in my life. It would be a story for the book I wrote if I ever actually got down to writing it, and I'd get to go in a limo and see lots of cute guys in suits.

"Valentina?" He made a face and took a step toward me. "I thought you guys weren't really friends."

"Well, things changed." I shrugged and looked away. I knew that he and Valentina had hooked up last winter. Josh had been back home in Colorado for the winter break, and Valentina had been skiing in Vail, and somehow they'd met up and had sex. Valentina mentioned it every time she saw him. "I should ride Josh one more time," she'd say and then giggle whenever she saw him. "That boy's got some stamina." It made me feel like shit because for a few moments in time, I'd thought that Josh and I could possibly have something, but obviously he tried to get with every woman he could.

"Well, maybe we can go to a movie next week or something?" He offered me a winning smile, and I shrugged.

"Maybe." I stepped away from him. "I have to go shower now. Have a nice night, Josh." Disappointment crossed his face, but I ignored it. This was a man that had made me question if I had the ugliest vagina on earth and that was why he'd fallen asleep.

I hurried toward the shower room and tried not to think about that evening with Josh. Maybe he'd fainted because he'd been shocked by all the hair down there. Maybe I would use the cream, after all. Even though I knew it wouldn't matter. I wasn't that desperate that I'd drop my panties for any man that flirted with me. Even if he was a hottie in a suit. I couldn't remember the last time I'd seen a man in a suit.

As I stepped into the bathroom, I determined that I was going to have a good night tonight. I'd push myself out of my comfort zone. Maybe I'd even have my first make-out session under the stars. Maybe my mystery suited man would bring me glasses of champagne and wine and we'd dance in the moonlight. I knew I was totally getting carried away, but it was nice to dream. In romantic movies, parties like this always led to something amazing. They always led to you meeting the love of your life or some gorgeous stranger that swept you off your feet. I wasn't meeting many guys at school. Well, that wasn't true. I was meeting boys, but I was ready to meet men. Someone like Colin Firth if Colin Firth was still in his early twenties.

I started to feel excited as I headed toward the showers and turned on the water. I was grateful that there was no one else in the room right now. I closed my eyes and thought about the night. I was going to a ball. I was like Cinderella, only it was going to be a good time because I had a real invitation and I didn't have to leave at midnight. The driver would take me home whenever I wanted to go. If it absolutely sucked, I'd leave in an hour and I'd tell Valentina that she owed me big time and would have to take me to brunch or something. Brunch was always fun. She could afford to take me to a real nice place as well.

Not that I would want her to spend all her money on me because that wasn't who I was, but I was saving her relationship, which was big. Even though I hadn't even realized she was in a serious relationship. I chewed on my lower lip as I dropped my clothes to the floor. I was starting to feel anxious again.

My emotions were mixed about the upcoming evening. A voice in the back of my head told me I was too nice and that I should just stay home. The devil on the other side told me I'd never have a life if I always stayed home. The angel whispered back that I could hang out with Josh, but the devil whispered back and asked me did I really want another opportunity to embarrass myself? Josh falling asleep between my legs right before he was going to go down on me had been mortifying. Especially seeing as he was the first guy I'd even let have access to me in that way.

I grabbed the soap and rubbed it against my skin. The water was slightly too hot, but I didn't turn the temperature down. I felt like if I was going to play with fire, I might as well get used to the heat.

I knew I was an overanalyzer, and I also knew that I didn't know Valentina that well. Valentina didn't seem like the sort of woman that would settle down or get serious with someone in college, but I knew I was judging her because she was beautiful and seemingly had it all. She was a tough cookie to crack. I knew nothing about her, really. She was mysterious and beautiful, and I was slightly envious of the fact that she had made New York City her own, even though she'd grown up overseas from what I'd gathered.

I had grown up in New York, and I still felt like I was a foreigner in the city. Sure, I knew my way around back alleys and streets that most people never went down, but I'd never experienced the magic of the city that fabulous people got to experience. I didn't go to exclusive parties and bars. I didn't mingle with the who's who of fashion, art, or the business world. It was just me and my dad, my grandparents, and my friends, and we stayed in our small little bubbles, which was nice in its own way, even if it had grown to be very boring. Even with my dad having worked for the mayor, nothing eventful ever happened in our lives. I was a part of the most boring family on earth. Sometimes I wondered how different my life would have been, if my mother had still been alive.

I took a deep breath and pinched myself. "You can do this, Callie. You are going to have the best night of your life, and you will not regret it," I mumbled to myself, trying to convince myself that that was going to be true because I really, really needed for this to be the start of a brand-new life for me. Maybe I'd meet the man of my dreams. Maybe I'd meet my Prince Charming. And he'd sweep me off of my feet and take me to live in a castle somewhere. I grabbed my razor and started shaving my legs. Maybe his lips would be filling my calves with kisses this very evening. I knew I was delving into fantasyland, but a girl had to have some dreams.

CHAPTER 5

Antonio

"Oh, God," said Monte Cristo, *"your vengeance may sometimes be slow in coming, but I think that then it is all the more complete."* — Alexander Dumas

Dozens of maids flittered around the country house, getting it ready for the party to start. The first guests would arrive within an hour. Surprisingly, I wasn't feeling tense, though I knew it would hit me sooner rather than later. I stared at the black suit carefully laid on the bed by Luisa, the old housekeeper that escorted my father everywhere he went. She was as dutiful as a dog and knew all of the family secrets. Sometimes I didn't wonder if she had a few of her own.

"Antonio, I have your cravat." Luisa's melodic

voice entered the room as she knocked and walked in without waiting for a response. "It's Valentino."

"Thank you." I took the silk gray tie from her. It was patterned with what appeared to be buttons. It was the ugliest tie I'd ever seen in my life.

"Your papa got it for you." She stared at me. "It cost six thousand euros. It was shipped from Italia." That was her way of telling me I had to wear it. Luisa was like a bulldog when it came to my father. She would see no one disrespect him. She was more trustworthy than Tommasso was to my father. And Tommasso was his righthand man.

"I will wear it." I nodded as I waited for her to leave. Instead, she walked over to the large chest of drawers that was pressed up against the wall and ran her finger across the top, checking for dust. I studied her plump frame from behind. Her graying hair was in a neat bun on top of her head, not a hair out of place. She was wearing a long, black dress that did nothing to flatter her figure. Her shoes were also black and flat: ugly and boring. She turned to look at me, her eyes watching me warily. They were her best feature. Bright blue, keen, and piercing. They stood out in her face, which might have been pretty when she was younger. She was matronly in appearance, but in personality, she was mean. She had raised my brother and me after my mother had died. And even though my father had remarried, none of his wives

had taken on a motherly role. Not that Luisa had
been motherly. She'd been strict and cold and insistent on us always respecting our father.

I somewhat believed she was in love with my
father. That she'd seen her role as our de facto
mother-in-law as some sort of honor.

But my father would never look at the likes of
her. Not when he had young, thin, blond bimbos
willing to worship him at every opportunity. Not
that Luisa had saved herself for my father. She had a
teenage daughter, Elisabetta, that had been sent off
to a boarding school when she was young and came
home every summer for two weeks. Though I hadn't
seen her in a few years, not since she was thirteen.
Alessandro thought that whoever Elisabetta's father
was, he must have broken Luisa's heart and that was
why she didn't like to be around her. Elisabetta
looked nothing like Luisa; she'd been a beautiful
child and obviously resembled her father, whoever
he was.

"Antonio," Luisa spoke softly, and her face
contorted slightly. "I have known you all your life."
She paused dramatically and if she were anyone else,
I would have seen that silence as a threat.

I nodded for her to continue. I had an idea of
what she was about to say. It would be repetition of
the same speech my father had been giving me all
week. She'd tell me to choose a woman that fit into

the family, that would know her place, that would know how to rule alongside me. That love was the last thing that mattered. I was starting to get annoyed at how everyone was talking to me. As if the only thing holding me back from marriage was looking for a true love. The thought was laughable.

"Find a woman that can keep your secrets." She stepped toward me, her fingers grasping the crucifix around her neck. "Find a woman that can love you." She stopped in front of me. "You don't have to love her, but she has to love you." She reached up and touched the side of my face. "I am not your mother. I have not loved you as a mother. I have loved you as a woman who knew you would grow to be king of our world. Perhaps I was not kind. Perhaps I was even cruel at times. You are cold. You are your father's son." She sighed. "I have regrets, but my life has passed now. I am paying for my sins."

"Luisa." I touched her hand softly, surprised at her words. "What are you trying to say?"

"You are your father's son, yes, but you have your mother's eyes." She frowned. "A silly wisp of a woman, but she was kind."

I wanted to slap her for talking about my mother, but I never hit women. I lived by a code. I did not physically hurt women or children.

"I have to change," I snapped and turned around, pulling off my shirt and flinging it to the ground.

"I know you don't want this, Antonio." She spoke

softly. "But it will happen. Just remember, make sure she loves you. If she loves you, she will do anything to protect you. No matter what you do, she will be by your side. I know you don't believe it exists, but a woman in love will cross all lines for the man she loves." I turned to look at her then, and I could see tears in her blue eyes as she rubbed her crucifix. "I'm not a good woman, but I have done everything for a reason."

"You're not a bad woman, Luisa." She hadn't scarred me, even if she hadn't been warm toward me or Alessandro.

"Elisabetta." She sighed. "She deserved better."

"You did what you thought was best for her."

"Yes." She nodded. "But she is headstrong. She will find it hard to find a husband."

"You're not hoping I will marry her, are you?" I inquired of her. Was this where all this was going?

"No, no." She shook her head and frowned. "I must go." She hurried toward the door. "Just remember, Antonio, they call you the wolf for many reasons. Not all of them are bad." She exited the room without another word, and I closed the door behind her. I locked it and then walked over to the windows and pulled the light-blocking curtains shut. I then turned off the lights until I was standing there in the dark. It was silent, aside from the ticking of the clock on the bedside table. I was hovering on the line that existed between dark and light. I was living in the shadows. I was the shadow.

"Il fine giustifica i mezzi," I whispered under my breath. *The end justifies the means.*

I was ready.

CHAPTER 6

Callie

"I love you as one loves certain dark things, secretly, between the shadow and the soul." — Pablo Neruda

The limo ride was smooth and exciting, and I only wished I had someone to share it with. The driver had pointed out bottles of champagne and wine for me to consume, but I'd stuck to mineral water. I wanted to have all my faculties with me at the party, so I didn't mess up anything. The red dress and heels that Valentina had commanded me to wear were in a small black duffel bag on the seat next to me, along with a small case full of makeup. Valentina hadn't had time to do the makeover, after all, so had just handed me what she'd called essentials: foundation, concealer, powder, blush, bronzer, mascara, eyeshadow, eyeliner, lipstick, lipliner, and then a matte spray for when it was all on. I had no idea the order in which to apply everything, but I'd figure it out.

I'd decided to wear my favorite paid ripped jeans and NYU sweater in the car so that I'd feel more comfortable. I half hoped that the party wasn't as formal as she'd let on and that I wouldn't need to change into the dress, after all. I took another large sip of water and sat back in the plush leather seats. The driver was playing opera music, which added to the intensity of the moment and the drama in my head. The female singer sang with passion, and I suddenly wished I understood Italian. I wondered if Valentina spoke Italian. I wasn't even sure if that was her heritage, but I figured it might be.

"We're about twenty minutes from the manor, Ms. Romney," the driver's voice informed me via the intercom.

"Thank you," I said, wishing I'd been allowed to sit in front next to him. I was dying to have a conversation with someone, anyone, about what was going on. I grabbed my phone to text my dad. It had been a few days since we'd talked, and I knew he was frothing at the mouth to hear from me. He'd called me five times, left three voicemails, and sent seven texts. I'd been mad at him because he'd ordered a new bed for me in anticipation of me moving back home after college, but that was the last thing I wanted to do. My dad had been overprotective all my life, but I was ready to spread my wings and leave the nest. And he just didn't want to let go. There were so many things I hadn't done in life because of him. The first was turning down Stanford University in California so I could go to NYU and stay closer to home. I almost felt like I still lived at home because I saw my dad every week for dinner.

"Ten more minutes, Ms. Downey."

"Thank you," I said into the darkness. I shimmied my butt down the seat and stared out the window. We weren't in the city anymore. Darkness surrounded the car. I could barely make out the silhouette of trees, and an ominous feeling filled me. I looked back at my duffel bag, and a million thoughts clouded my mind. "What the actual fuck am I doing?" I mumbled as I texted my dad. **Love you. I'll call you tomorrow.**" Which I hoped I would actually be able to do.

I didn't even know where I was. Where was I going? For a few seconds, the thought crossed my mind that I was going to be a human sacrifice. I watched far too many horror movies and sometimes my mind got completely carried away. The limo came to a sudden stop then, and I noticed we were at some gates. The manor was literally in the middle of nowhere. What sort of party was this? Four burly men in suits walked around the limo, and I noticed they all had prominent guns in holsters on their hips. What the hell? I was starting to think that I'd made a huge mistake.

The limo driver had a conversation with one man for about five minutes, and then the wrought-iron gates opened, and we continued on our way. I was grateful that the security guards hadn't looked in the backseat. They would have known immediately that I didn't belong at this shindig.

The limo came to a full stop next to a Mercedes and a bright-red Ferrari, and I swallowed hard. This party was full of rich people. I was going to stand out like a sore thumb. I suddenly wished that I wasn't such a nice person. I suddenly wished that I'd told Valentina that I wouldn't attend the party for her. It wasn't like she was my best friend. She didn't even know my major and most probably not even my last name.

"Welcome." The driver opened the door for me; his face was impassive and void of emotion. "The ball awaits, ma'am. I hope you have your glass slippers." I wasn't sure if that was his attempt at a joke, but he wasn't smiling.

"I sure hope the limo doesn't turn into a pumpkin at midnight," I said as I grabbed my bag, but he didn't respond. "By the way, what was the opera you were playing? I loved it."

"*Carmen.*" His eyes gazed into mine for the first time. I took it as a sign of approval at my question. "It was composed by Georges Bizet."

"Oh, amazing." I nodded, trying to pretend that this wasn't the first time I'd ever heard of him while also being thankful that I hadn't said something like, "I love Mozart."

"I just love the Italian language." I beamed at him, and my heart sank as his lips pressed together and he looked away.

"That was French." He slammed the door shut.

"Oh." This conversation had been a fail after all. "Well, it was great." My voice trailed off. He was already walking away from me. I assumed he knew to wait for me. He was my ride back, it was the middle of the night, and there didn't appear to be any nearby trains or buses, and I certainly didn't have enough money for an Uber.

"Lucia, wait up," a woman next to me called out to a blonde about ten yards in front of us. She stopped, turned around, and frowned at her friend.

"Maria, please walk faster." The brunette next to me stumbled forward in what appeared to be four-inch heels. They were both absolutely gorgeous in their long ball gowns and sleek updos. Diamonds glittered off of Lucia's long, dainty neck. I wondered if they were real. There was no way. She didn't look any older than I was, and I had no jewelry to talk of, save for a ring that had belonged to my mother when she was younger. And I never wore it because I was scared I would lose it.

I clutched the duffel bag closer to me as I looked

around and took in my surroundings. The manor before me was grander than I'd initially thought when the limo had pulled in. The front of the house was adorned with ornate balustrades and grand marble columns that encompassed the entire front of the building. Ivy climbed the walls in the most dignified of ways, and pink and red rose bushes were illuminated by the lights that spotlit every guest that walked inside.

Elegant women in evening gowns and glittering diamonds were escorted from luxury cars and limos, and I noticed all of them were accompanied by men in dark suits. Every single man had an inscrutable expression on his face. Some of them even resembled mean bulldogs, and I wondered where the hell I was.

I walked toward the entrance and realized I needed to change quickly. My ripped jeans and over-size NYU sweater would stand out like a sore thumb. Without even thinking about what I was doing, I found myself pivoting direction and heading to the side of the house instead of the entrance. I figured I could find some bushes to hide behind to change my clothes. It didn't sound like the most comfortable of changing rooms, but it was better than strolling up to the front doors looking like the help. In fact, even the help was dressed better than I was. No one would believe I was Valentina in my current attire.

"Shouldn't you be inside?" A jovial male voice made me freeze. Was he talking to me? I ducked back against the side of the stone house but soon realized the voice was talking to someone else.

"Kick rocks, Alessandro," an annoyed voice answered back. I watched as two tall men came into view. They had their backs to me, so I couldn't see them well. I pressed into the cold wall behind me, hoping the shadows would protect me from being discovered. The duffel bag strap felt uncomfortable on my shoulder, but I didn't dare adjust it.

"Now now, big bro." The man on the right laughed. "Or should I say, Prince Charming?"

"Knock it off." Whoever big bro was didn't sound amused. Their faces were covered by the thick brush next to them, but I made out the silhouette of his arms raising as if to throw a punch.

"We should have a fairy tale commissioned for you." Alessandro's voice still held humor. "We'll call it 'the day the big bad wolf became the white knight.'" A scuffle broke out, and my jaw dropped as the other guy pulled a gun out and cocked it at him. "Chill, bro!"

"This situation is ridiculous," the angry guy shouted. "Like I have time for this bullshit." He lowered his gun, but my heart rate still raced ten miles a minute.

"You didn't say no, though."

"I have my reasons."

"You always do. Now put your gun away before I take it from you."

"You couldn't if you tried." I pressed my palm against my mouth, scared I'd let out a shocked whimper. Both men looked poised and ready to pounce, like Jaguars about to attack their prey. Was I about to witness a murder?

Oh shit, oh shit! My heart was racing, and I wanted to close my eyes, but they wouldn't shut. How could I explain witnessing a murder in the countryside to my dad? He would kill me. I had to get out of there before I became a witness to something that could have me in witness protection.

I started to move as unobtrusively as possible when a stupid branch decided it wanted to see me dead. CRACK! I froze as the two men turned around, their faces on high alert as they ran over to me. So much for blending in with the house. *"Hush little baby, don't say a word, momma's going to buy you a mockingbird."* The sweet, gentle tones of my mother's voice filled my head, and I was grateful for the sound as it helped me regulate my breathing.

"Oh, hi." I waved nonchalantly, looking around like I was a tourist observing the gardens at Versailles. "Nice evening for a stroll, am I right?" *Do not faint, Callie.*

"What?" One of the men approached me, his eyes dark in the night.

"I was just admiring the gardens." I swallowed

hard as he grunted. This was definitely the angry man that was a little too gun happy. He was not smiling.

"Roses and dandelions are my favorites," I continued as I waved around me. My heart thudded loudly, and the sound of an owl hooting rang ominously through the night sky. That was a sign. I was about to die. "And lilies," I mumbled to fill the silence. I looked around me quickly; it was so dark on this side of the house that you could barely see the gardens, let alone any flowers. Another fail for the night.

"Are you here for the party?" The jovial man approached, a warm smile on his face. That must have been Alessandro, the joker that had nearly lost his life.

"Yes," I squeaked out, directing all my attention at him. "My name is Valentina." The lie came easier than I thought, which surprised me. Maybe I was good in tense situations, after all.

"Nice to meet you, Valentina. What family are you from?" He leaned against a tall oak tree that I thought seemed to be way too close to the house. Wouldn't the roots ruin the plumbing? *Focus, Callie!*

Alessandro's body looked lean and deceptively languid, and I wished I could see his face. His sense of humor made me want to get to know him better. I wished the angry man would disappear. His attitude was starting to get on my nerves.

I stared at Alessandro blankly for a few seconds. What family was I from? What was he talking about?

"Not the Windsors, obviously," I tried joking. "Harry is married now, so I lost my chance."

The men just stared at me, and I suddenly wished that bad jokes weren't my go-to when I was in uncomfortable situations. They'd never really helped me, and it certainly didn't look like they were about to start now.

"You're hardly dressed to impress," the angry man said. There was a sneer on his face as I looked over at him. Whoever he was, he was a jerk. I decided not to answer him. I would be a woman of mystery and play it cool.

"So you just decided to stroll in the gardens before you went inside?" He sounded skeptical, and I didn't blame him. Every other woman was rushing to get inside to party.

"Well, I have this book I'm reading." I reached into my duffel bag to grab it but soon realized that I had made a mistake when they both pulled their guns on me.

"Oh." I swallowed hard, grateful for the darkness so they couldn't see my face burning. My heart was racing, and I felt like I was about to pass out. I'd never even seen a gun in real life before, and now, here I was in a dark, vast garden with two men I couldn't even identify, and for all I knew they would rape and kill me. Or steal me and make me a sex slave. I wanted to lose my virginity, yes, but not that way. Nervous giggles escaped me as I stood there. I wanted to slap myself for my off, awkward, and sometimes dark sense of humor.

"You think this is funny?" The sneering man pressed his lips together, and I tried to see him better, in case I needed to identify him in a lineup. "Do you want to die?"

"No," I squeaked out. I held my hand up with the paperback I'd brought with me, just in case the party had been dull. I should have known that Valentina would never have been invited to a boring party. *"And Then There Were None."* I waved the book in air. "It's the book I'm reading. By Agatha Christie. She's a famous British crime writer…" My voice trailed off as the man chuckled. His brother stood behind me, something akin to disbelief on his face. I guessed not many women brought books to parties.

"I know who she is," the angry man said, and they both put their guns back in their holsters. Though I noticed that angry man still kept his hand on his gun. "You studying for a life of crime?"

"Oh no," I said quickly, just in case they thought I was here to case the joint and steal from the owners. "I abhor crime and criminals. I think that most criminals are the scum of the earth."

"I wouldn't say the scum." The joking brother laughed. He gave his brother a look I couldn't quite make out, though I could see my comment had made them more at ease. Maybe they really had been worried I was a thief trying to steal jewels in the night. There did appear to be a lot of rich guests. Maybe these two bozos were security guards. I didn't think so exactly, but I wasn't about to ask and clarify their role at the party either.

"Anyway, I was just enjoying this beautiful night. Look at the moon and the stars. I think that might be the seven sisters constellation." I pointed up. "You would never see that in the city." I realized I was mumbling then and most probably losing their interest. Why couldn't I be one of those women that knew how to flirt? Why couldn't I tell a sexy joke and have a coquettish laugh and suggest a quickie in the grass before we went in? Not that that was something I wanted to do, but even though I could only really see the silhouette of their faces and bodies, I could tell they were fit and quite handsome.

"You shouldn't be out here," the angry man growled at me, and for a few moments, I wondered if he'd turn into a werewolf or something right there in front of me. I'd read *Twilight* and been Team Jacob, but now that the possibility of me being Bella was real—if only in my mind—it no longer seemed so romantic. I didn't want to be with a werewolf. Or even meet one.

"I don't want to mate," I said under my breath, and the man took a step forward. I gasped as I saw his features for the first time properly in the moonlight. He was gorgeous. Mean, with a brooding face, but absolutely panty-dropping gorgeous.

"What did you just say?" His light brown eyes gazed into mine, a sinister veil surrounding his irises that made me shiver.

"Uhm…you're not related to Jacob or Dracula, are you?" I wanted to groan inside as I stared at his lips. I had no idea who this man was, but I was very interested in being pressed up against the wall for one brief, hot kiss, if only to satisfy my need for a romantic adventure. Alessandro burst out laughing, and the angry brother just stared at me. There was an intensity in his dark gaze that made me shiver.

"I think you better get inside." He lowered his voice, and I swore he almost growled again. "You really don't want my fangs out, little lamb, because I might draw more than blood."

I gasped at his words, not knowing what he meant and not wanting to find out. Well, that was a bit of a lie. A little part of me was intrigued. A little part of me wanted him to push me back up against the cold stone wall and devour me in ways I couldn't even count. It was a weird feeling to be slightly turned on in such a situation, but I really was. I stared at him, jutted my chin out, and poked him in the chest.

"Trust me, you don't want to know what my fangs would do in response," I said quickly before running away from the two men and back toward the front of the house. My breath came quickly as I stopped by the front door, and I was almost positive I could hear a howling laughter in the shadows from where I'd come. I didn't know who those two men were, but I hoped never to see either of them again.

CHAPTER 7

Antonio

"In revenge and in love woman is more barbaric than man is." — Friedrich Nietzsche

There were two hundred women standing in the room and one hundred and ninety-nine of them were staring at or talking about me. I didn't care about any of them. My eyes were searching for her. The woman in the ripped jeans, dirty white Converse, and oversize NYU sweater. She'd said her name was Valentina, and we'd both known she'd been lying. She had no idea what was going on tonight. Or who I was. She was the one woman in the room that didn't even know who I was. I smirked, wishing I could see her face when she found out. When she realized who I was. She'd regret her words to me. I couldn't believe she'd asked me if I was Dracula, though as I'd stared at her bare neck, there had been nothing I'd wanted to do more than caress her. But we were strangers, and for all her backtalk, she wasn't used to men like me.

"Why do you look like the cat that just got the canary?" Alessandro was by my side now, his eyes skipping across the room to see if anyone caught his fancy.

"I won't appreciate it if you sleep with my bride before me." My voice held a warning, but my eyes were smiling as I looked over at him.

"Tell me which one you want, and I'll choose between the others." He grinned and then let out a low whistle as the Gambino twins walked past us, giving us indecent eyes in their even more indecent gowns. To anyone listening in, they would think he was joking, but I knew better. Alessandro would sleep with half the women there, all in one night if he could. My brother was a lover, in all senses of the word. He didn't do monogamy. Though we were different in most ways, we were both confirmed bachelors. Our mother's untimely death had seen to that. Neither men nor women could be trusted in our world. And if I was honest, there was no one I trusted one hundred percent implicitly besides Antonio. Life had a way of hardening men in our world. I loved him more than anything, and I knew we would take a bullet for each other, but there was no one else I would risk my life for.

"Why don't you choose who you want first?" I laughed. I already knew who was top on my list, and my brother wouldn't have paid any attention to her. He liked women that were done up, with their faces plastered in makeup, flash jewelry, fake nails, big boobs, and empty brains. NYU girl fit none of those requirements.

"I don't know." The smile dropped from his face, and there was a tinge of regret in his tone. I studied his profile for a few seconds, contemplating his countenance. "The band is great." He pulled a cigar out of his pocket. "We should dance and get this party started." The fleeting moment of sadness that had washed over him had passed. Whatever had crossed his mind was now gone, at least from public view. But I needed to get to the bottom of it. Something was bothering Alessandro, and I'd had no idea.

"You go ahead. I need to mingle. Say my hellos. There are far more prominent families here than I thought." I stifled a sigh. The evening was going to be boring at best. I hated having to make small talk.

"You are The Wolf, dear brother." Alessandro's tone was dry. "Everyone wants a piece of you, even those that hate you."

"I don't know why I'm surprised to see the Valentis and the Giordanos here after what went down last year."

"I assume the Valentis want their turf back." He shrugged, not even worried about the threat of a gunfight. "We kicked the Valentis out of Queens completely."

"The last thing Pietro told me was that he'd blow my head off if he saw my fucking face again." My right hand automatically went to my gun. "You don't think he's here for a fight, do you?"

"All Pietro Giordano wants is for his daughter Ana to suck your balls and be your wife." My brother laughed, delighting in his own crassness. "He'd let you fuck her tonight if you promised it would only be up the ass." He winked. "She'd still be *pure* and a virgin on your wedding night."

"Alessandro, sometimes I think you become more and more of a pig every single day." I chuckled as I shook my head. Though what he said was true. It was important, in our world, for women to be pure on their wedding night. This was for two reasons. Most of us were still good Catholics, if not by deeds, then by words. The other was for respect. A mafia boss demanded a virginal wife as a sign of respect. I, personally, thought it was bullshit, but then I didn't make the rules. I also didn't intend on actually following through with the wedding, but no one had to know that just yet.

"A sexy pig, though." He smoothed his shirt down. My brother was not short on self-confidence. Which wasn't surprising, as he was a good-looking guy. Some said he was even better looking than I was. His eyes roved the room, and he froze for a few moments. I shifted my stance to see what had gotten his attention. His back was stiff, and I could see his hands balled into fists. A woman in a sleek silver dress was looking back at us, and I lifted my hand in a wave as I saw her.

"Oh, look, it's Gia," I said, wondering how Alessandro would feel knowing his former best friend was here in competition to become my wife. "Wouldn't it be funny if I ended up marrying her?"

"Oh?" he asked dismissively as he turned away. "Good for her. Oh, look, Bambi Alessi is waving for me to come over. I'll chat with you in a bit." He hurried away as if he didn't have a care in the world, and I filed his reactions into a folder in my head labeled "Alessandro." He and Gia had been friends for years, and the friendship had ended a few years ago. I'd assumed amicably, but I'd never asked why. It pissed me off that there may be beef there that I didn't know about.

The boss had to be all-knowing. And if Alessandro and Gia had fallen out for bigger reasons that just growing apart, I needed to know.

"Antonio, wanna get out of here?" Jimmy, one of the made men in the family, approached me. Jimmy was one of my best friends, loyal to the end. He was my main enforcer when stuff was going wrong in the businesses. He and Alessandro were the only two I trusted most of my secrets with. Besides my two cousins, Carlo and Lorenzo, but I knew ultimately the two brothers would always choose to protect each other in a fight, whereas for Jimmy and Alessandro, I was number one.

"You know I can't leave right now," I said and then laughed as he pulled a small, black leather flask out of his back pocket and chugged the cheap whiskey inside. "We have booze, Jimmy."

"You got fucking girly drinks—champagne and vodka." Jimmy chugged again and offered the flask to me, his blue eyes alight with mischief. Jimmy resembled a young Frank Sinatra with his bright blue eyes, jet black hair, and scrawny build. However, his size was deceptive. He was one of the strongest men I'd ever met. He had a deep Brooklyn accent and constantly got into arguments, but the women loved him. Other men often assumed he wasn't a threat when it came to a fight, but Jimmy could shoot a target in the bull's-eye with his eyes shut. He was also loyal to a fault; he was like the third Marchesi brother, only he wasn't. He knew his place. His dad had run one of the gambling dens for my dad but had died in a shootout with one of the Irish mobs, when he was just a kid. He'd grown up with his aunt and uncle but had spent a lot of time with me as teens, as we'd both frequented the boxing ring on an almost daily basis. All-in-all, Jimmy was good people.

"Tony, you want a swig or not?" The flask dangled in front of my face. I was about to decline when instead I grabbed it and drank two mouthfuls myself. The liquid burned as it went down my throat and settled into my stomach. This was the sort of alcohol that made you a man. Or an alcoholic. Lucky for me, I was already the former and had no interest in being the latter.

"The cheap shit again?" I rubbed my forehead as I felt my father's gaze on me. I knew he was telepathically telling me to make the rounds and not hang out with "that fucking loser, Jimmy," but I didn't care.

"You don't pay me enough to buy anything else." He grinned, and I just rolled my eyes. "I gotta get outta here in an hour or so. That redhead's on my balls and wants to see me tonight."

"You like her?" I raised an eyebrow. Jimmy didn't catch feelings or usually run to be with women.

"I like the way she sucks my—"

"Antonio," the soft, dainty voice of Ana Valenti interrupted Jimmy, and I was grateful for it. I didn't care to hear Jimmy go on about the virtues of his latest bedmate.

"Ana." I smiled and leaned forward and kissed both of her cheeks. "You look radiant this evening." And she did. Her dark eyes shone, as did her long, dark hair. Her dress was a midnight blue that clung to her every curve. She was stunning.

"Thank you. You look as handsome as ever." She stared directly into my eyes. "But I suppose you already know that." It wasn't a question. I could sense the bitterness in her voice. Ana Valenti hated me as much as her father did, but for different reasons.

"How is the family?" I asked her softly, attempting to avoid a minefield. There were too many women in here that I had history with. Women I'd bedded, women who wanted me to bed them, and women that wanted me to fall in love with them. I'd heard rumors that many women in our world wanted to be the one to crack through my shell; somehow they still believed in fairytales. They believed that the dark knight could become a prince charming. I didn't want to remind them that in the original fairytale, the wolf had eaten Red Riding Hood.

I had no interest in falling in love. I had no heart. I had no wish to become one with any woman. I had left a trail of broken hearts, and I didn't care. I didn't look backward. Only one thing drove me now. Ana responded to my question, but I wasn't listening. My eyes were roving the room, looking for Little Miss Coed. She wouldn't rush over to me with big eyes, begging me to love her. She wouldn't try to convince me to make her my wife. She didn't even know who I was. She intrigued me. I wanted to talk to her again. I only hoped she hadn't already left.

CHAPTER 8

Callie

"I seem to have loved you in numberless forms, numberless times, in life after life, in age after age forever." — Rabindranath Tagor

I felt dreadfully uncomfortable in the dress. It was too tight and slightly too small. The zipper at the back didn't go up all the way, so I'd let my hair loose instead of keeping it in the cool chignon bun that Valentina had told me to wear. I hoped my hair would hide the fact that the dress didn't fit properly and hide the top of my exposed back. I walked out of the room I'd ducked into to change feeling uncomfortable.

The shoes were pinching my toes. I took a deep breath. "It's going to be fine, Callie," I mumbled, trying to convince myself that I was going to have the night of my life. Just because it had already started horribly didn't mean that it couldn't get better. The two random men I'd seen in the garden had put me off a little bit, but I doubted I'd see them again tonight. I passed a hallway mirror, and my jaw dropped at my reflection.

The red dress was stunning. The bodice was skintight, showing a huge expanse of the top of my breasts, which made me slightly uncomfortable, though I had to admit they looked good. The cinched waist made me appear slimmer than I was, and the skirt flowed out like red flames. My hair hung down my back in loose waves, and as I walked up to stare at my face, I realized I hadn't done too badly with all of the makeup. My brown eyes glowed, and I could see specks of green. The bronzer shimmered on my cheekbones, making my face appear slimmer, and my lashes looked long and lush. My lips were a bright red to match the dress, and I smiled at myself. I looked hotter than I'd ever looked before. I twirled around in the corridor, pretending that I was dancing with some hot man. A door slamming brought me back to earth, and I headed toward the staircase.

I stared down and saw that the entryway was packed. The entire house was packed. And the house was humongous. I crept down the stairs, trying to be as unobtrusive as possible. There were at least two times the number of women as there were men, each one more glamorous than the last. All of them were beautiful. No one was even paying attention to me, which I was glad for, though slightly dissatisfied. Even though the dress didn't fit perfectly, I thought I looked good, but no one had even glanced at me. I'd have to remember to take a photograph to send to my friends before the night was done. No one would believe that tonight I looked like Miss America when I barely ever got out of a sweater and jeans.

"Oh, no," I said as I stumbled forward down the last few steps. I'd been so busy thinking about my appearance, and I hadn't been paying attention.

"Are you okay?" a girl asked as she reached out a hand to stop me from falling flat onto my face.

"Hi. Yeah, I'm just a little bit clumsy; the heels are a bit tricky to walk in. Thanks." I stared at her. She was gorgeous with her oval blue, almost purple, eyes and long, black hair. She wore a silver dress that seemed almost like liquid silver on her body.

"No worries," she said. "I hate heels as well." She wrinkled her nose and looked down at her own tall stilettos. She took a couple of deep breaths as she pressed her lips together.

"Hey, is everything okay?" I asked her, concerned.

"Yeah, I was just rushing out of the main ballroom, and I guess trying to run in heels in this dress doesn't always work well, you know?" She laughed and fanned her face. "I'm a bit hot and bothered right now."

"Yeah, I get that," I said, nodding. "This is some event, huh?"

"Oh, yeah. This is some event, all right." She frowned slightly as she stared at me.

"I don't recognize you," she said suddenly, looking me up and down, her eyes narrowing as she tried to place me. "I feel like I would've remembered you."

"Oh," I said, biting down on my lower lip. Was I really that out of place at this event?

"Yeah. I mean, all the families know each other." She giggled as she looked around at the women milling past us into the main ballroom.

I blinked at her. So I hadn't imagined it. What was going on with all these families? Who were all these families?

"Yeah," I said and then wrinkled my nose. "Do you mean like the royal families, or…"

She burst out laughing then. "You're funny."

"Oh, thanks." I wasn't sure what I'd said that was funny, but I wasn't going to ask.

"I'm Gia, by the way," she said, offering her hand.

"Oh, hey, I'm Valentina," I said quickly, my face growing pink with shame. I didn't like lying, but I knew there was no way I could tell her my real name was Callie, because what if other people came up to me and I had to say Valentina? Then she'd say, "I thought you told me your name was Callie." And I'd be like, "Well, some people call me Callie, and some people call me Valentina." And well, that just wouldn't do.

"Nice to meet you, Valentina," she said, her eyes still searching my face. "So are you here because you have to be, or are you hoping to win the prize?"

My eyes lit up for a second. Prize? I hadn't even gotten a raffle ticket. Shit, what if it was something great like $10,000 or a Mercedes or something? There were enough fancy cars parked in the driveway that they could afford to give one away for free.

"I didn't even know about the prize," I said, thinking that honesty was the best policy in this situation. "Do I get a ticket from one of the security guards or..."

She blinked at me. "You are funny, Valentina. Are you trying to be a comedian?"

She grabbed my hand, and I let her hold it as she escorted me into a side room. There were only about five women in there and two men standing by the doors, both in black suits. These men looked rougher than the men I'd seen in the garden. In fact, without the suits, they looked kind of thuggish. One of them had tattoos all over his face, and the other one was sporting a black eye. I wouldn't like to see either one of them late at night in an alleyway.

"So Valentina, what do you do? Where do you live?" She leaned into me as if we were old friends.

"I live in Manhattan," I said quickly. That was the

truth. "Well, I used to live in Brooklyn. My dad's in Brooklyn, but I'm in Manhattan now."

"Oh." There was a puzzled look on her face.

"Oh, what? Where do you live?"

"I'm in Manhattan, and I thought I knew everyone in all of the families around my age. How old are you, if you don't mind me asking, of course?"

"I'm twenty-one. You?"

"Same," she said, frowning slightly. "What do you do? Or are you the oldest in your family, and they're waiting for you to marry?" She paused. I didn't know what she was talking about, but I shrugged.

"I'm at NYU. I'm studying psychology and English, and well, I guess I want to save the world one day. I don't know. I'm still deciding what I want to do when I graduate."

"Oh, cool." She laughed. "I'm at Columbia. I live on the Upper West Side."

"Wow. That's cool. You must be rich," I said, staring at the glittering jewels that adorned her throat and wrists.

She laughed. "My family does okay. I'm guessing that your dad is no longer well-regarded if I've never heard of you." She looked around.

"Yeah," I said, not knowing what she was talking about. "What do you study at Columbia?" I wanted to change the subject before she figured out I was a big liar. Hopefully, my nose wasn't growing.

"I'm studying history, which is ironic because it's

not like I can become a college professor or anything."

"Oh, why not?"

"Well, I'd have to have my master's or PhD before I could do that."

"Aren't you going to apply, then?" If her family was rich, she could definitely afford it. She looked at me with wide eyes.

"You know I can't apply. A bachelor's is as far as we can go."

I was the one to look puzzled then. I had no idea what she was talking about.

"Come, let's go to the main ballroom," she said. "I need a glass of champagne."

"Oh, that sounds nice," I said, nodding, following behind her. I was grateful to have met Gia. She was friendly and nice, and even though she fit in aesthetically with the crowd, she didn't seem snooty like the other women. I'd already seen some people look me up and down like they thought I was trash, which I didn't appreciate.

As we made our way into the ballroom, my jaw dropped. Three humongous crystal chandeliers were hanging from the ceiling. On the far end of the room, velvet curtains were hanging with long, gold-tasseled drawstrings. Upon the walls sat paintings of many different famous artists that I recognized: Picasso, Monet, Dali, and Rembrandt. They couldn't possibly be real, could they? Waiters were gliding around the room with gold trays in their hands, offering chutes of champagne and canapes to the guests. "Come on," she said. "Let's get some *champagne*," she said in a French accent, and I giggled. Gia was fun. I hoped we could be friends after this event, and then maybe when she came to the dorm, I'd introduce her to the real Valentina and explain why I'd had to lie, and hopefully, she'd forgive me.

"Thank you," she said to one of the waiters as she grabbed two glasses and champagne and handed me one. I took a sip. "Oh my gosh. This is delicious." I swallowed hard, enjoying the smooth, slightly sweet beverage. "Wow."

"You've never had champagne before?" She looked surprised.

"I have, but it's never tasted as good as this. This must be the good stuff."

She took another sip and shook her head. "It's okay. I wouldn't say it's the best champagne I've ever had."

"Oh?" I was surprised.

"Yeah, I mean, it's not an $8 grocery store bottle or anything." She giggled. "But it's not top shelf."

"Oh, I'm used to the $7.99 bottles," I said honestly. She blinked at me, and her expression changed slightly as she leaned forward in a conspiratorial fashion.

"Can I ask you something, Valentina?"

"Sure," I said, with a nod.

"Was your dad a soldier?"

"Huh? You mean like in the army?" I asked her. Her eyes stared at me in confusion for a few seconds.

"You don't have to be embarrassed. I mean, I know there's a hierarchy, and soldiers and made men are at the bottom, but just because my dad's a consigliere doesn't mean that..."

"Oh no, my dad wasn't a soldier," I said. "Why?" I had no idea what she was talking about. Soldiers, made men, consiglieres. Was consigliere another term for a prince or viscount I had never heard of before? I had thought I was well-read and cultured, but maybe I just didn't know the terms for the very rich.

"Oh, hello, Gia," a high-pitched voice interrupted our conversation. I looked up and stared at a pair of twins, both of them with identical expressions of superiority on their faces. They looked at Gia, then they looked at me, and then giggled slightly as if they saw something funny.

"Hello?" Gia said, nodding dismissively. "So as I was saying, Valentina, I was thinking that..."

My jaw dropped. I was surprised that Gia was being so rude as the two girls were still standing there.

"Hi, I am Valentina," I said quickly, offering my hand.

They both looked at my offered hand, looked at each other, giggled, and walked away.

"Don't mind them," Gia said. "They're ridiculous."

"Oh, okay," I said. I watched as they walked away and looked back at us with derogatory stares.

"Yeah, both of them want Antonio, and I'm sure they'd kill the other one for a better chance."

"Wow." I assumed Antonio must have been some hot guy that they were both after unless she was talking about Antonio Banderas, the actor. I didn't think she was because he had to be at least sixty and married. And, well, that didn't exactly make him an eligible bachelor.

The hairs on the back of my neck suddenly stood on end, and I felt a shiver run down my skin. He was looking at me; I just knew it. As sure as I knew my own name, I knew that the angry man from the garden's eyes were upon me. It was weird. I'd always read books where the protagonist said they could feel someone staring at them, and I'd never experienced it before. In fact, I hadn't believed it could be true. How could you feel someone staring at you? But in that moment, I felt eyes upon me. I looked up and around the room. There were so many people in here. There had to be at least two hundred different women. And then I saw him, the man from the garden. His eyes were on me, staring intently, a brooding expression on his face. His brows were furrowed and his expression was dark, but my heart skipped a beat. The room was bright, and I could see his face and body better now. He was, for want of a better two words, fucking gorgeous.

I quickly looked over to Gia to see if she had noticed the man practically glaring at me, but she was looking at something on her phone. I couldn't stop myself and looked back to see if he was still looking at me, and he was. I didn't understand why. Did he know I was a fraud? Was he going to tell the host? I bit down on my lip. What if he had me escorted out of the party by a bunch of security guards? The two twins would loudly proclaim that they'd known as soon as they'd seen me that I was a fraud.

"So, Gia, what made you come to the party tonight?" I asked her, my voice shaking slightly.

"My father made me, of course." She wrinkled her nose. "I assume that's why you came. However, I can't see Antonio being with a daughter of a soldier or a made man. Sorry. I don't mean to say that." She stepped forward and touched my arm lightly. "You seem lovely and all, but…"

"Hey, Gia, can I ask you something?" I cut her off, my brain close to blowing up.

"Sure," she said. There was a wistful expression on her face.

"What are you talking about?" I bit down on my lower lip. "I know I should most probably know what this party is for, but I don't, and you keep saying things that are confusing me, and while I don't want to expose myself for being ignorant…"

Her lips pressed together, and she pulled out her lipstick from a small clutch at her side. I watched as she reapplied the deep red to her lips, and then she leaned forward with a wicked glint in her eyes.

"You really don't know what's going on, do you?" She sounded delighted.

"No," I said, shaking my head.

"And your name's not Valentina, right?"

"No. Don't tell anyone, please. She's my roommate and begged me to come here tonight, and my real name is Callie." The words rushed out of me, and I was grateful to finally be able to tell the truth.

Gia nodded as if she'd known all along, and then she lowered her voice. "This is a bride selection party, Callie."

"A what?" I almost screeched. It was my turn to sound and look confused. "A bride selection party?"

"For Antonio Marchesi." She stood back as if that should mean something to me.

"Antonio Marchesi?" I asked, still confused. "Who is he when he's at home?"

"You've never heard of the wolf?" She shook her head, her eyes looking more purple now. "Wow, you really are clueless. He's the underboss to the entire Marchesi family, the largest mafia syndicate in New York City."

"No way." My jaw dropped. "This is a party for a mafia boss?"

"Yeah, Callie. This is a party for him to choose his wife. Whoever he decides he wants will have to marry him."

That's when my heart dropped. The reality of the situation finally hit me. I was at a party for the mafia. What was I doing here? I had no business being here. Not only was I not Valentina, but I also didn't want to marry a mafia boss. I didn't know what was going to go down if he found out I was lying. I didn't even know who he was.

"Hello." The deep, dark, familiar voice sounded from in front of me, and I looked up. I hadn't been able to see his eyes properly when we were in the garden, but now the man I traded stinging words with was standing in front of me, his brown eyes dancing with mischief, his lips a thin line.

"Oh, hi," I said. Trust him to come up to me right when I'd just found out that news.

"Who are you?" he asked me softly.

"Sorry, what?" I said, swallowing hard. Not this crap again.

"I said, who are you?"

"Valentina," I squeaked out, and then because he was annoying me, I repeated my words in a stronger tone. "My name is Valentina."

He stared at me for a couple of seconds, and then

he stared at Gia and shook his head before stepping forward and whispering in my ear.

"I think we both know that's not the truth." His breath felt like a caress as his tongue lightly touched my earlobe. I jumped back in shock, and he laughed, a deep, unforgettable sound that didn't reach his eyes. "Who the fuck are you?"

CHAPTER 9

Antonio

"To take revenge halfheartedly is to court disaster: Either condemn or crown your hatred." — Pierre Corneille

Her face was trembling as she stood there. Her eyes shone with fear, and I could see her looking around the room, as if she were trying to determine an escape plan. Silly little lamb, did she really think she could run away from me? She was a fraud. And she'd gatecrashed my party. She had to know that wasn't acceptable.

"I will ask you one more time." I reached for her wrist and held onto it tightly. It was dainty, though she was stronger than I thought as she yanked it back away from me. How I wished I'd had handcuffs in that moment. She would have fallen to her knees in shock if I'd handcuffed her.

"What is your problem?" Her other hand pinched me, and I chuckled slightly as I released her.

"My problem?" I looked at her and then at Gia, who was being decidedly close-lipped. "How are you, Gia?"

"Fine, thank you."

"Why so formal? We're practically siblings." I stared at her hard face. She was mad at me. Whatever had gone down with Alessandro was obviously still affecting her as well.

"Not quite." She rolled her eyes. "Not anymore."

"Look, dude, I don't know your obsession with me, but we were having a conversation here." The fake Valentina was getting brave now, and I stifled a smile.

"I think that perhaps you do not realize who you're talking to."

"What?" She rolled her eyes. "Let me guess, you're Don Juan."

"Not quite." My eyes roved her body. The dress fit her nicely. Red was definitely her color. I thought of the red lingerie I had in my room. I wouldn't mind seeing her in that. Only then, I'd be able to see more than just the tops of her breasts heaving. I'd see her bare nipples as well, hard and eager. Waiting for me to kiss and touch them.

"Stop." She glared at me, her face red.

"Stop what?"

"Looking at me like that."

"Like what?" I raised a single eyebrow and stared deep into her eyes. She looked nervous and slightly turned on. I withheld a grin.

"You know."

"I have no idea." I shook my head and then leaned down and whispered in her ear. "Unless you're talking about the fact that my brain is wondering what you look like without that dress on."

She gasped and stepped back. "You are rude." She shook her head. "I have a mind to make a complaint about you and then you'll be in trouble."

"With whom?" I asked her, curious if this was her way of threatening to call the police.

"The mafia boss." She gave me a pointed look. "He's my close friend."

"Uhm…" Gia touched her arm, but I gave her a look. She wrinkled her nose at my command but kept quiet.

"He's your friend, is he, *Valentina*?" The words dripped like honey from my mouth. I was a Venus flytrap beckoning her in.

"Yes." She nodded and looked around. "And you're going to not like what he says or does, when…" Her voice trailed off, and she frowned slightly. Gia was shaking her head imperceptibly, and I sighed. I wanted this little game to continue for a little longer. I was quite enjoying myself.

"Gia, go and get us some champagne please," I commanded her, and even though she wanted to protest, she didn't. Gia knew our world. She knew you didn't say no to an underboss. She walked away without saying anything, and then I lightly tapped my fingers against my upper thigh. I could see eyes on me around the room so I knew I couldn't do exactly what I wanted to do in that moment, which was a pity.

"You really think you're God's gift to women, don't you?" The Valentia wannabe looked angry. "I don't know who you think you are, but—"

"But you want to know, don't you?"

"No." She shook her head. "I couldn't care less."

"You will." A sinister smile crossed my face.

"Doubt it."

"I know it, my dear." I ran my fingers down the side of her face, and she froze. "I think that this moment will be burned into your brain for the rest of your life." It suddenly struck me that if we were in a room alone, I'd quite like to brand her, mark her as mine. I'd only do that if she let me, though. I wondered how she'd feel knowing she couldn't get away from my imprint. They didn't call me the wolf for no reason. I took what I wanted. I possessed what was mine. And she was going to be mine.

"You think a lot of yourself, but I doubt I'll even remember you in five minutes, let alone tomorrow or any other day."

"Liar," I whispered but then froze as I saw my

father approaching. What would he say when he saw her? Would he know she wasn't meant to be here?

"Antonio, there you are." His voice was annoyed. He didn't even glance at her. He didn't care. I let out a sigh of relief. "Come, I need you to meet someone."

"One second, Papa." I looked back at Valentina, and her face was ashen. She finally understood who I was now. The corners of my lips twitched as she realized who she'd been mouthing off to. "Yes," I said under my breath. "I am Antonio Marchesi, the mafia boss you said you know so well. And when I get back, I want some answers from you, little lamb, because we both know that you're not Valentina." I ran my fingers across her trembling lower lip and then blew her a kiss before walking away. I didn't have to look back to know she was shaking in her boots.

CHAPTER 10

Callie

"The greatest happiness of life is the conviction that we are loved—loved for ourselves, or rather, loved in spite of ourselves." — Victor Hugo

"Whatever you do, do not let anyone know that you're not me."

Valentina's words rang hollow in my head as I glanced around the room. Antonio had walked away for a couple of minutes, but I knew he wasn't done with me. There'd been a glint in his eyes as he'd stared at me, an almost mocking look.

I bit down on my lower lip. My heart was flooding, and I felt completely out of place. This was not the world for me. Yes, I'd wanted an adventure, but not quite like this. I had to get out of here. I knew Valentina wouldn't be pleased that I hadn't stayed long, but at least I'd arrived, and at least I hadn't blown her cover. I had a lot of questions to ask her. One, why didn't she tell me it was a party for a mafia boss, and two, how did her dad know these people?

I could hear the light giggles of two girls next to me whispering something about Antonio and his brother Alessandro. It seemed to me that most of the women here were more than eager to marry Antonio, and I didn't understand why. He didn't seem like he'd be particularly romantic. He certainly wasn't sweet or nice or anything I was looking for in a boyfriend. In fact, he seemed mean, and full of himself, and cocky, and the list could go on and on. Granted, he was handsome if you liked that brooding, sinister look.

Gia walked over to me with another glass of champagne and offered it to me. I took it from her hesitatingly.

She frowned slightly. "Are you okay?"

I shook my head. "I think I got to get out of here. I don't feel comfortable."

She stared at me for a couple of seconds and then nodded. "You really are a fish out of water, aren't you?"

"I guess I am," I said.

"Look," she said. "You're not going to be able to get out of the front. All of the soldiers and made men are guarding the doors until the official announcement."

"The soldiers and made men?" I raised a single eyebrow at her. I had no idea what she was talking about.

She laughed slightly. "Sorry, I keep forgetting you're not from our world. With your dark hair, you look like you could have Italian heritage."

"Yeah, I get that all the time." I nodded. "But I'm not. My dad, his parents are from England and my mom…" I took a deep breath. "Well, she was from South America. Her parents were."

"She was?" Gia asked me, a question in her eyes.

"She passed away when I was just a baby," I said. "She died of cancer."

"Oh my gosh. I'm so sorry." Gia reached over and touched my hand. "That's devastating."

"Thanks. I was so young that I don't really remember her. Just a song she used to sing me when I was younger. It's weird because sometimes it will just pop into my brain and I don't even know why. My dad said that she wrote it for me. She wanted to be a singer-songwriter." I shrugged. "But anyway."

Gia pulled out her phone for a couple of seconds. "You're cool, you know that?"

"Thanks," I said, surprised.

"What's your number?"

"Huh?" I stared at her in confusion.

"I want to get your number so we can catch up out of here seeing as we both live in the city, and then I'm going to help you figure out a way to get out without anyone noticing."

"You'd do that for me?"

She nodded. "Of course. If I could get out of here without anyone noticing and my parents killing me, I totally would."

"You're really sweet."

"I don't know that I'm sweet, but I like you and I want to help. Plus I know the Marchesi men." She rolled her eyes. "You don't want to get mixed up with either of them."

"Oh?" I asked her in surprise. I hadn't thought she was that familiar with either one of them. "You and Antonio?" I asked her, a pause in my voice.

"Oh no." She shook her head. "No. I used to be best friends with his brother Alessandro."

"Oh, okay. Used to?" I prodded. I knew I was being nosy, but it seemed like there was a story there.

She rolled her eyes and wrinkled her nose. "Yeah. Used to, but I don't want to get into it."

"Okay," I said. "Well, my number is 917-121-3234."

"Perfect," she said as she typed it into her phone. "I just texted you so you'll have my number."

"Great," I said.

The lights dimmed in the room suddenly, and I froze. "What's going on?" I asked her.

"They're about to have the big announcement," she said in hushed tones. She leaned forward.

"So Antonio's dad is Roberto Marchesi. He is the don, and if you don't know what that means, he's the head of the entire Marchesi family in New York City. It's most probably the largest mafia family in the United States right now. They definitely have the most money. That's why even though this ball is super unconventional, there are so many different families represented."

"Oh?" I asked, not really sure what she was saying.

"So in mafia families, it's not like royalty or anything. We don't have selection balls like you see in Hallmark movies. Normally the families get together and a match is chosen. Usually from a suitable family. However, for Antonio Marchesi, they're doing it slightly different."

"Why is that?" I said.

"I don't know," she said, shaking her head. "Most probably because it's the only way he would agree to find a wife."

"Oh?" I raised an eyebrow. "He's not into women?"

That surprised me because the looks he'd given me had certainly made me feel like he was sizing me up in more than one way. And the way my body had responded and tingled, I knew that I was attracted to him even if I didn't like him.

"Oh, he's straight," she said, laughing. "He's most probably fucked half the woman here." She shrugged. "Well, maybe not half, but a lot. But he's not the sort of man that one would expect to get married. He's not cool. He's not sweet or loving or…"

I nodded emphatically. "I can totally see that. He seems really mean."

"They call him the wolf for a reason," she said and bit down on her lower lip. "Anyway, I think his dad's about to make an announcement." She shivered slightly. "His dad gives me the creeps."

"Oh, why is that?"

"Well," she said in hushed tones. "They say he killed his first three wives."

"No way." My jaw dropped.

"Yeah. So Antonio's mom died in a car crash when he was young. They say it was because Roberto wanted her dead. She was going to leave him. She'd fallen in love with someone else."

"Wow," I said.

"And then his second wife disappeared on vacation in some country in Asia."

"What?"

"No one knows what happened to her, and she's presumed missing and dead. And then his third wife, well, she fell off a cruise."

"She did not fall off a cruise."

She nodded. "Yep. They say she was sleeping with

one of the drivers. And now, well, who knows what's going to happen with his fourth wife?"

"Oh, wow. Did he love them all terribly?"

She burst out laughing then. "Roberto Marchesi love? He doesn't love anyone but himself. That's why Antonio and Alessandro are so…" She sighed. "Well, anyways, that's why they have issues. Hey, we better get you out of here while the lights are still dim. Come with me."

She grabbed my hand, looked around quickly, and then we made our way to the exit. Two security guards stared at us.

Gia gave one of them a winning smile. "Hi, Salvatore."

"Hello, Gia," he said.

"We're just going to the restroom to freshen up."

"Okay." He nodded. "But hurry, the don's about to speak."

"We will," she said, sweetly. "Come on, Valentina."

"Coming," I said, nodding at him and hurrying behind her.

She led me up a hallway and grabbed my hand. "You got to go faster than that. Come on."

"I'm coming. I don't know, but I feel nervous right now."

"I get it," she said. "But we don't have any time to spare."

We hurried up a long staircase and then down another long, dark corridor. I was starting to feel a foreboding as we made our way into a dark room. She turned on the light, and I blinked. We were in some sort of study. The walls were a dark gray wallpaper. The floor was a dark purple mahogany wood, and there was a large Persian rug in the center. On each side of the walls, there were bookcases adorned with hundreds and hundreds of books. To the far right, there was a large wooden table with some papers and a nice leather chair.

"This is really nice," I said. "I'd love to look at these books and—"

"Come on. We don't have time," she said. She hurried over to the window and opened it. "There's a tree there."

"Okay." I blinked at her, not quite sure what she was saying.

"You're going to have to Pollyanna it."

"Pollyanna it?" I stared at her in confusion.

"Yeah, you're going to have to climb down the tree and escape."

"I can go out the back or something."

She shook her head, her eyes wide. "No, this is the only way. There will be soldiers everywhere. You don't want to get caught. You don't want to get taken to Antonio. He'll figure out pretty quickly that you're not Valentina, and then, well, I don't know what he'll do. He might think you're a spy or an undercover agent with the FBI or something."

"I'm just in college," I said. "I can't believe I agreed to come to this party."

"It's okay." She smiled at me and rubbed my shoulder. "You'll be fine. We're only three stories up. Just climb down the tree, go to your driver, and leave."

"Okay." I nodded. I gave her a quick smile and hug. "Thank you, Gia. It's really nice of you to help me."

"Don't worry about it," she said. "But I better go. They'll be wondering where I am. I know how Alessandro will have his eyes out looking for me."

"Oh?" I asked her questioningly.

She shook her head. "Don't want to talk about it. Good luck."

"Bye," I said.

"Ciao," she said and hurried out of the door.

She turned the light off and then closed it behind her. I stood there in the darkness, looking at the tree and staring at the sky. It was pitch black outside, save for a sprinkling of stars and a full moon.

I bit down on my lower lip. I didn't want to climb down a tree. I wasn't the most athletic of people, and I certainly wasn't going to be more athletic wearing a dress and heels. And then I remembered, I'd left my duffel bag in one of the rooms. I didn't know if I had time to go and get it. I had my clutch and my keys and my phone, but I didn't have my book or my jeans or my sweater.

A loud dong sounded through the entire house then, and I froze. An owl was hooting outside the window, and I knew I had to make a decision. I didn't have time to go back and get my duffel bag. It wasn't worth the risk. I had to leave.

I stared out at the oak tree next to the window. It was a far way down, but I knew I had to do it. I had to try, and well, if Pollyanna had been able to climb down a tree, certainly I could as well. I'd been a bit of a tomboy when I was younger. Granted, I had never been one for climbing tall trees, and I didn't like heights, but I'd have to risk it. I couldn't afford seeing Antonio Marchesi again. I couldn't afford for him to find out I wasn't Valentina. I didn't want to get mixed up with the mafia.

I took a deep breath, took a step forward. "Here goes nothing," I mumbled under my breath and crossed my fingers as I reached for the branch closest to the window.

CHAPTER 11

Antonio

"Revenge is the raging fire that consumes the arsonist." —
Max Lucado

"Daddy says that as I'm his daughter, and he's your father's consiglieri, that I should have a really good shot at being your wife." Serena giggled slightly and pressed her hands against my chest.

I stared at them disdainfully. She didn't seem to notice.

"I think I'd like to be your wife, Antonio. You could tie me up with—"

"Not now, Serena," I said dismissively.

I looked around the room, frowning. Where had the girl that was calling herself Valentina disappeared to? I could see my father walking toward the center of the room ready to make his speech. He'd be passionate. He'd have everyone smiling and clapping. Not because what he said would be so dazzling, but because they knew if they didn't, there was a good chance he would take some sort of action against them.

"Antonio, if you want us to go to the back room, I could…" she said.

I looked down into her eyes. "I said not now, Serena."

I brushed past her and walked along the periphery of the room. I could see everyone's eyes on me, wondering who I was going to pick. It was unusual, definitely, for a mafia underboss to have an event like this, but I hadn't heard too many complaints.

I walked up to Salvatore, who was standing by one of the doors. "Have you seen Gia and her friend?"

Salvatore looked at me for a couple of seconds and nodded. "They went to the bathroom."

"I see. Thank you."

I was about to head out of the door when Salvatore touched my arm. "Your dad's about to speak."

I looked at him, and he dropped his arm quickly. He knew better than to touch me.

"And I have something to do," I said, cold faced. "I already know what my father's going to say, and I don't really need to be there to hear it."

"But you—"

"But what, Salvatore?"

"Your father told me to ensure you stay in the room."

I stared at him, considering for a couple of seconds. "And what are you willing to do to ensure that I stay?" My finger rubbed my thigh softly.

He blinked. He knew what that meant. "Nothing, sir. Sorry."

I stared at him, nodded and left the room. I could see Gia hurrying back down the stairs, her face blushed.

"Hello, Gia. Where are you off to?"

"I'm going back into the room to hear your father's talk," she said quickly.

"And Valentina? Where is she?"

Gia gave me a warm smile. "I think she's still in the bathroom," she said, shrugging.

"Okay."

Gia wrinkled her nose. "She'd kill me for saying this, but I think maybe the shrimp canapes were off. She's had a dreadful stomach, and I've given her some Imodium, but I don't think it's worked yet, if you know what I mean."

I stared at her for a couple of seconds and nodded. She didn't blush. She didn't look like she was lying. In fact, her face was warm and open, which was the clue that gave me away. Gia was no longer warm and open toward me. When her friendship with Alessandro had busted up, she'd taken on an air of cold indifference toward both of us when-ever we saw her.

"Thanks," I said as I continued up the stairs.

"Where are you going?" She blinked. I heard a stutter in her voice.

"I'm going to grab a new tie," I said, looking down at my perfectly good black tie. "Wanted one with a bit more color. Give me a bit of pizzazz, you know? I am the groom-to-be, after all."

She licked her lips. "Oh, okay."

"Why? Would you like to come with me, Gia?" I gave her a warm, seductive smile. "Perhaps you'd like to choose which tie I wear."

"No, I think not," she said.

I could see her swallowing hard as the front of her throat dropped slightly.

I took a step toward her. "Are you sure?" I whis-pered close to her ear, my eyes gazing into hers.

"What's going on?" Alessandro's voice was deep. He had also exited the room. I turned to look at him and rolled my eyes.

"Nothing. Gia and I were just having a private conversation."

"About?"

"None of your business," Gia said, shaking her head and running all the way down the stairs. She brushed past him without a glance and into the room.

Alessandro headed toward me. "What the fuck was that about, Antonio?"

"I just asked her if she was interested in becoming my wife," I said, staring at him. "Why? Would you have a problem with that?"

"You're not going to marry Gia," he said, shaking his head.

"And why is that?" I asked him, a single eyebrow raised.

"Because she's too good for you."

"She's too good for me? The underboss of the Marchesi familia?" I stared at him. "I think you don't know what you're saying, dear brother."

"I think you know exactly what I'm saying, dear brother." He shook his head. "She's off-limits."

"Who are you to say who's off-limits?" I chuckled slightly.

We stared at each other for a couple of seconds, and he rolled his eyes. "You know you're not interested in Gia, Antonio. You've known her practically all her life."

"Yes, and maybe that's why she'd make a good wife," I said softly. "She knows exactly who I am, and she won't have any expectations that won't be fulfilled. And I do believe she's still a virgin," I said, licking my lips. "We'd definitely have those bloody sheets to show the day after the wedding."

His eyes grew cold as he stared at me, and I wondered what he would say or do next. Alessandro was my brother, and he respected my authority over him, but I knew sometimes he was close to being on the ledge. I knew sometimes he wanted to usurp my authority. Not because he wanted the power, but because he didn't agree with things I said or did.

"You can do whatever you want," he said. "I'm headed back into the room. Papa's about to start talking."

"Fine," I said. "I'm just headed upstairs."

"For?" he said.

"To change my tie."

"To what, another black tie? What's really going on?"

"The woman in the garden, I think she might be upstairs going through our things. I wanted to check on her."

He stared at me for a couple of seconds. "You really think she's going through stuff? She won't be able to get anything important."

"I know." I nodded. "But she's certainly not Valentina."

He started laughing then. "Very funny, brother. We both know she's not Valentina."

"Exactly," I said. "So I need to have a conversation with her before she departs."

"Gia was with her?" he asked me, a sudden light in his eyes.

I nodded. "She most probably took her to the study."

"Okay and?"

"There's a tree there. You know the one by the window?"

"Yeah, and?"

"When we were younger, we used to climb down it all the time when we wanted to escape."

"Escape?"

"You know, when we wanted to go and do stuff without having a watchful eye on us."

"I didn't know that happened."

"Exactly, because we never went through the front or the back doors. We went down the tree."

I stared at him for a couple of seconds, finally understanding what he was saying.

"You said it's by the study?"

He nodded. "Go around the side. If she's going to be anywhere, she's going to be under that window."

"Thanks, bro," I said, nodding.

"You're welcome." He chuckled. "What would you do without me?"

"I don't know," I said. "Perhaps I'd have a lot more of a quiet life. Now you head back inside. If Papa asks for me, tell him I'm on my way."

"Okay." He nodded curtly and headed back into the room.

I made my way back down the stairs and toward the front of the house. Two of our main men stood there, ensuring no one left.

"Hey, I'm just heading out for a second. I'll be right back."

"Yes, sir." They nodded, not even blinking as I made my way through the front door.

As soon as I got down the front steps, I ran toward the side of the house and back toward where the oak tree stood next to the window. Gia was smart. She knew that if this girl was going to leave, she couldn't do it through the front or back entrances. She'd have to find another way. And then I saw the window was open and I saw a figure in a blood-red dress holding onto the tree for dear life.

I smiled to myself. "Well, well, what do we have here?" I said as I made my way slowly toward the base of the tree.

I wouldn't let her know I was there, not until she landed, and then I'd demand some answers. I leaned back against the cold stone wall of the house as she tried to shimmy down.

One of her heels fell, and she yelled. "Oh shit," she moaned loudly, obviously not knowing anyone was there.

I could hear fear in her voice. She had to be at least twenty feet high, and it didn't seem like she was accustomed to climbing trees.

"Okay, you got this," she mumbled under her breath as she climbed down to another branch. "Why me?" she moaned out loud, and I shook my head. She certainly wasn't one to keep quiet.

"Ah!" she said, screaming suddenly as her foot missed a branch, and she came falling down. I stepped forward and held my hands up to grab her.

"Ah no!" she screamed. The sound carried through the night sky like the cry for help that it was. I couldn't stop myself from grinning. I couldn't have crafted a more perfect moment if I'd tried.

I caught her right before she hit the ground.

"Ah?" She blinked as she looked up at me, and I held her close to me. Her body was soft and warm against my own hard torso.

My eyes were dark as I looked down into her face. Her beguiling eyes looked back at me, big and brown and nervous. I could feel her heart racing as she was still pressed against me. She stumbled slightly forward and her hair cascaded around her face. For a few seconds she reminded me of a cherubic angel—all sweet and innocent. But then I remembered her pretending to be Valentina and trying to escape in the dark of night. She wasn't that innocent.

"Who are you?" I said softly. "And where are you going?"

There was a veiled threat in my tone as I stared at her. My fingers gripped into her waist. She stared back at me for a couple of seconds, blinking. She swallowed hard. There was a look of defiance in her eyes as she gazed back at me. Her chin tilted up just a little bit, as if challenging me to get the information from her.

"I said who are you?"

"Nunya," she said, wrinkling her nose at me.

"Excuse me?" I brought her closer to me.

"Nunya," she said, tilting her chin up higher.

I withheld a laugh. "Okay, Nunya. Do you know who I am?" I smirked. I pressed my lips close to her ear, loving the feel of her trembling body against mine. Her voice was strong, but her body was weak. She really was foolhardy to be talking this way to me. Didn't she know men had lost fingers for less insolence? She seemed educated, so she had to know she was playing with fire. So then this was a game to her? The fact somehow delighted me.

"I don't care who you are," she said, trying to push away from me, but I wouldn't let her go. My grip was like a vice. "Let me go," she said.

"I don't think so, Nunya."

She bit down on her lower lip to stop it from trembling. Her fingernails dug into my biceps, and I flexed them as she tried to hurt me.

"I am Antonio the wolf Marchesi," I said softly. "This is my party." I looked around our surroundings. "You're trespassing on my family's property."

"First of all, I'm not trespassing." She said quickly. "I know this is your party, and I'm not interested in you," she said, blinking quickly.

I started laughing then.

"You're not my type."

I raised a single eyebrow. "Well, we both know that's a lie." She stared at me in confusion, and I smirked. "I'm everybody's type."

She rolled her eyes. "Wow, you're so full of yourself."

I didn't say anything in response to that. "Why are you trying to leave? The party's just begun."

"I'm not interested in this party," she said. "I don't want to marry you."

I started laughing then. I couldn't stop myself. "Do I have Alzheimer's?" I said, scratching my head. "I don't believe I asked you to marry me." I leaned back into the wall. "Don't tell me I fell, bumped my head, and forgot I asked you to be my lawfully wedded wife?"

She shook her head defiantly, her eyes annoyed as they gazed into mine. Her face seemed unsure as she gazed at me. She was beautiful. Unlike the other women I knew. She wasn't done up professionally or reserved. She didn't hide what she was feeling. Which wasn't a good trait for a member of the familigia, but she wasn't a part of our world. "That's not what I'm saying. I know this is a party for you to find a wife, and I'm not interested. I don't want to be with you."

"You do like lying, don't you?" I said softly. "Now tell me your name."

"No," she said obnoxiously, pushing against me

again. I felt her raising her knee and I pushed it back down hard. She didn't really think I'd let her knee my in the crotch, did she? Though I liked the idea of her walking across me in just her heels. I wondered how she'd react if I told her that.

I was starting to get irritated by this game of cat and mouse. "I can get the answer out of you the easy way or the hard way," I said softly. "What's it to be?"

"What's the hard way?" she said, pushing against me again, her palms soft against my chest.

I laughed at her weak struggles. My grip tightened on her waist, and I brought her closer to me.

"What are you doing?" she said, panicking now.

"You said you wanted to learn the hard way." I grinned at her, and I felt myself hardening.

Her face blushed. "That's not what I meant."

"Come with me." I grabbed her hand and pulled her alongside me, as I moved back along the side of the building. We could spent the entire evening going back and forth and I didn't have the time. Not when Papa was inside waiting to introduce me to several hundred women that would love my attention on them. Attention that this college coed liar was receiving.

"Where are we going?" she said. "I want to go home."

"Really? And why do you want to go home?"

I looked down at her long, flowing hair, her

heaving bosom. The red dress was sexy and suited her. And all I wanted was to see it on the ground.

"Because I want to go to bed," she said.

My lips twisted up. "Oh, is that an invitation?"

"No," she said quickly. "I mean alone."

I chuckled. No woman had protested this much around me in a very long time. "Come."

"Where are we going?" she said. Her voice was softer now as I dragged her back toward the front of the house.

"You'll see."

"But I…"

"You what? You still haven't told me your name."

"It's Valentina," she said softly and then started coughing. Even her own body was betraying her lies.

"We both know you're not Valentina." I blinked at her. "You might like lying, but you're not very good at it."

"What?" she said, looking down at the ground.

We made our way to the front of the house. The two soldiers glanced at me and glanced at her and nodded.

"I'm just going to be upstairs," I said. "If anyone's looking for me, tell them I'll be down momentarily."

"Yes, sir." They nodded.

I held her hand tightly and grabbed her toward the staircase. "Let's go."

"But where are you taking me?"

"To my bedroom," I said and then leaned down

and pressed my lips against her hair. It was soft and silky against my face. I breathed her in. She smelled like roses on a rainy day. Her scent was intoxicating.

She stilled as my lips made their way to whisper in her ears. "I'm taking you to my bedroom, sweet little lamb."

"But I don't want to go." She pulled away from me, and I laughed and shook my head.

"We'll see what you want when we get there, Nunya."

We continued up the stairs, and then we came to a long hallway. I made a right and walked into a solid wooded door with a cast iron knocker. I closed the door behind us and locked it before letting go of her hand.

"You can't keep me in here," she said. "You can't lock me up like this. You are going against my fundamental rights as an American citizen. This is…" She tried to open the door as she shouted into the room. Her eyes were wild as she gazed around, searching for something. I assumed she was looking for a weapon or object to use against me, but she wasn't going to find one. Not that I was planning on harming her in any way. That would be no fun.

I burst out laughing then. "Darling, no one cares that you're locked up right now and technically no one cares that…" I paused as I switched on the light. "Anyway, no need to fear, little lamb. You're not in my bedroom, so don't get too nervous and excited."

"I wasn't nervous, and I wasn't excited," she said. "You're a jerk, and..." She blinked as she looked around the room. "What is this place?"

"It's a special place for special people like you," I said with a small smile. I walked over to the table and turned on a machine. "This is a lie detector machine. I'm going to hook you up to it, and I'll ask you a couple of questions."

"What questions?" she said, her lower lip trembling.

"You'll see," I said. "I just want to know if you're lying to me or not." Which we both knew the answer to. She was a huge liar and not a very good one. But I liked playing with her. It was a bit like teasing a dog with a treat. I liked seeing her getting worked up. And unfortunately for her, I wasn't scared of her bite if and when she got fed up.

She bit down on her lower lip. "Why are you doing this?"

"I'm doing this because you've infiltrated a private party. You've pretended to be someone you're not, and then you tried to escape with who knows what." I shook my head. "Do you not know who I am?" I paused. "Oh yeah, I forgot. You don't care."

"I don't care. You're a brute. I am..."

"You're what?" I took a step towards her. She was unsure of herself. She knew what I was saying was true. This was obviously an invite-only party and she had not been on the official guest list my father had created.

"I'm going to call the police and you're going to be in so much trouble when they find out what you've done to me."

"You're going to call the police and say what exactly?" I stared at her through narrowed eyes. "You're going to say that you impersonated someone else, came to my party, snuck through my house, tried to escape, and when I caught you to figure out if you've stolen anything, you did not want to provide me with any answers. I think I know who the police are going to listen to and care about more." I shook my head. "I don't think you want to get charged for trespassing, do you?"

She stared at me with wide eyes. "I'm not trespassing, though. I had an invitation. I—"

"I don't recall inviting you, and it seems that you didn't really want to come to this party anyway."

"What are you talking about?" she said, shaking her head. "I'm wearing a dress and I never wear dresses."

"You just told me that you're not interested in marrying me. Correct?"

"Correct," she said, looking me up and down. "You're the last man on earth I would want to marry. You're a brute. You're—"

"Is that your word of the day or something?"

"What are you talking about?" She shook her head in confusion.

"You've called me a brute twice now, and I don't think I've done anything to you to be considered brutish." I chuckled. "In fact, I know I haven't because the truth of the matter is I can be a brute, but I've been nothing but nice to you, little lamb."

"Why do you keep calling me little lamb?" she said. "I'm not a lamb. I'm…"

"You're what? A pussycat?" I took another step toward her. I resisted the urge to pull her into my arms again. I didn't need her screaming.

She swallowed hard. "No, I'm not. I'm a woman, and…"

"And what?" I reached up and undid my tie.

She stilled then, her eyes widening. "What are you doing? What's happening here?"

"What do you want to happen?"

"Nothing." She shook her head, and I noticed she licked her lips nervously as she looked me up and down.

She was stunning standing there with her beautiful, chocolatey brown eyes and long, dark hair. She had an obstinate glint in her eyes, and I liked her spunk. I admired it even. I hadn't expected that.

She looked amazing in that dress. So different to the woman she'd been in the garden with her jeans and sweater. I swallowed as I stared at her tiny waist and her generous bosom. The dress was slightly too tight and clung to her. Her heels were tall, and the slit in the side of the dress accentuated her long, beautiful, slender legs.

I could imagine those legs wrapped around me, on top of me. Fuck, I was growing hard. I wanted her, but that was not part of the plan. I didn't take women that didn't want me, though I wasn't so sure that she didn't want me.

"Let's start again," I said in a soft voice. "Why don't you tell me your name and what you're doing here? And then if I like the answer, perhaps I'll let you go."

"You will," she said, biting down on our lower lip.

I nodded and gave her a warm, deceptively sweet smile. "Of course. I don't want to keep you prisoner or anything."

"Okay," she said, nodding. "Fine, but you have to let me go."

CHAPTER 12

Callie

"Let us be grateful to the people who make us happy; they are the charming gardeners who make our souls blossom."
— Marcel Proust

I could hear my heart racing. I wasn't sure what I was going to do. I was locked in a room with a mafia boss. The thought was preposterous. I didn't even understand what was going on. I stared at Antonio as he took a couple of steps toward me.

There was a look of compassion on his face, which surprised me because he didn't strike me as a compassionate man. His hair was short and dark and his brown eyes bright and vivacious. He had a very classically handsome face. He was possibly one of the best-looking men I'd ever seen in my life. He was almost beautiful, he was that good-looking.

I didn't know why he was throwing a ball to find a wife. He could essentially have any woman that he wanted, though perhaps the fact that he was in the mafia was not a positive trait to many women. I stifled a giggle, though I couldn't stop my lips from twitching.

"What's so funny?" he asked me.

My heart skipped a beat. This man didn't miss anything.

"Nothing," I said quickly, pressing my lips together.

"Your eyes lit up just now, and you looked like you wanted to laugh about something. I figure you're not laughing about this situation, so a thought must have crossed your mind." He cocked his head to the side and observed me. "I'm curious. What was that thought?"

He knew he had me cornered, and while I didn't particularly want to share my innermost thoughts with him, I figured what did I have to lose?

"I was just thinking that you're a good-looking man and you could most probably get any woman. But then it suddenly occurred to me that the fact that you're in the mafia wouldn't be a huge positive to most of the population, so that's most probably why you have this event tonight."

He didn't smile, and he didn't frown. He just continued to stare at me.

"You think that me being in the mafia is a negative trait?" His voice was stoic, and I didn't know what he was thinking.

"I mean, it wouldn't be a plus for me." I giggled nervously as he took another step toward me. "But obviously I don't speak for every woman. Maybe some woman like the fact that you're into a life of crime and murder and whatever else you guys in the mafia do."

His lips trembled, and he shook his head.

"So you think I'm a murderer and a criminal, do you?" He reached out and touched the side of my face.

I took a couple of deep breaths. I had no idea what he was going to do next.

"I mean, I'm sure you're not. You seem like a really nice guy." I knew I didn't sound convincing.

"Really," he said, chuckling. "Just a few seconds ago, you were calling me a brute and now I'm a nice guy?"

"Well, I mean, obviously I don't know you very well, but I can't imagine that someone with the nick-name The Wolf is particularly friendly and loving."

"So what is it, then? I am a brute that's unloving and unfriendly or I'm a nice guy that wouldn't hurt a fly?"

"I think we both know which one you are," I said, biting down on my lower lip.

"Do we now?" he said. His fingers moved to my lips, and he traced them roughly.

I could feel my stomach in knots and a strangeness between my legs. It was weird because although I didn't know this man and I didn't want to be in this situation, I found it oddly thrilling. That was most probably what came from the fact of only dating boys that didn't really seem to know what they were doing. This was a man, and not only was he a man, but he was also a powerful, strong, dominating man. Someone I'd only read about in books.

"So are you going to tell me your name?" he asked.

"It's Callie," I said quickly and let out a sigh. Valentina's going to kill me.

"So Callie, you admit you're not Valentina."

"Well, obviously," I said drily.

"You've got a lot of attitude for someone that's not in the best position right now," he said, moving his hand back and running it across his own lips.

I gasped as I saw him push his finger into his mouth and suck on it.

"You're wearing strawberry lip gloss," he said. "It tastes divine."

He grunted, and my entire body felt like it was going to melt onto the ground. I'd never experienced anything like it. We hadn't even kissed, and yet I felt close to this man than I'd felt any other man before in my life.

"Strawberry kiwi, actually," I said, smiling, trying to pretend he wasn't completely unnerving me. This was the sort of man I couldn't show weakness to. I didn't know how I knew that; I just did.

"Strawberry kiwi, then," he said. "Got it. So, Callie, why did you come instead of Valentina?"

"She's my roommate, and I guess her father wanted her to attend this event, but she had plans with her boyfriend Maksim, and I guess her dad doesn't like him. And she's kind of in this Romeo and Juliet situation, and I really didn't want to see them killing themselves because they couldn't be together. And she didn't tell me it was a party for a mafia boss. And she made it seem like it was going to be really fun and there were going to be a lot of hot guys. And she knew that I was kind of looking to meet a hot guy because my love life hasn't exactly been the best recently. And—" I paused.

He was laughing at me, not loudly, but his eyes were mocking me.

"Sorry. I ramble sometimes when I am slightly uncomfortable."

"I've noticed," he said, nodding. "But at least you're telling the truth now."

"Yeah," I said. "I mean, what do I have to lose? I don't want you to lock me up like I'm Rapunzel or something just because I gate crashed your party, which technically I didn't because I got in easily and no one even asked me to see an invitation."

"We wouldn't ask to see an invitation." He shook his head. "It doesn't work like that."

"Well, obviously, but maybe if you'd had invite only and people had to show their invitations, then this wouldn't have happened and you wouldn't have to accuse me of being an informant for the FBI or something, because I'm not. I'm just a college senior who thought I was going to get to go to a fun party and meet lots of hot guys, but it turned out not to be true."

"You don't think I'm handsome? Wait," he said, answering his own question. "You've already called me handsome."

"I mean, you're good-looking, but like I said, you're not my type."

"Really?" he said smoothly. "And why is that?"

"Well, for one, you're in the mafia. For two, you've not got the sort of personality I would really go for. And three, you're kind of older than me." In my head, I didn't care about his age. I'd do him in a second if he was someone else.

"How old are you?" he asked me softly.

"Twenty-one," I said quickly. "So yeah. How old are you?"

"How old do I look?" he asked, a smirk on his face.

"I don't know. Thirty-five?"

His smile left his face, and he shook his head.

"Really? I look thirty-five to you?"

I was lying, of course. He didn't look thirty-five. He didn't even look like he was in his thirties, but I wanted to bring him down a couple of notches. He was way too cocky.

"I don't know." I shrugged. "Forty?"

He pressed his lips together.

"Really?"

"What? You're a mafia boss looking for a wife. I don't know. How old do you get married in the mafia?"

"I'm twenty-seven, Callie."

"Oh, okay." So he was six years older than me. That wasn't bad. Six years was nothing. I'd totally date a guy six years older than me, not that I was interested in dating him. Plus, I was sure he wasn't interested in dating me.

"So have you got a number-one pick or anything?" I asked him.

He looked confused. "What are you talking about? Football?"

"No, for your wife." I shook my head. "Like, duh, this party is for you to find a wife, right?"

"Yes, it is. And no, I don't. If I had a number-one pick, I wouldn't have all these women here now, would I?"

"Oh, true." He was right, of course. That made sense. Any woman he chose would most probably run into his arms eagerly. I mean, half the women here were practically begging to become his wife.

"Why? Reconsidering what you said earlier?" he asked me softly.

"What did I say earlier?"

"You said you had no interest in the role."

"Oh, I don't," I said, shaking my head vehemently. "No, thank you. I do not want to be married to a mafia boss. I mean, my life is already kind of—" I paused.

"Your life is already kind of what?"

"I was going to say crazy, but that's not really true. My life's boring."

"So marrying me then wouldn't be such a bad thing."

"You don't want to marry me, though. I thought you had to marry someone from your world. That's what Gia was saying."

"I am supposed to marry an appropriate wife." He nodded. "In fact, that is what my father is telling our room of guests right now in the ballroom." He smiled. "It would be the best match if she were the daughter of a don or an underboss herself. A consigliere would also do."

"I'm sorry," I said, shaking my head. "But that doesn't really mean anything to me."

"Really?" he asked me contemplatively. "You know absolutely nothing about the mafia?"

"Yeah, I don't know anything."

"You've never watched a mafia movie or…?"

"No. No, ironically, my friend was trying to tell me to watch *The Godfather* the other day."

"Your parents have never mentioned the mafia?"

"Why would they?" I said, shaking my head.

"I don't know," he said. "You live in New York. We pretty much run the city."

"I don't know about that," I said, shaking my head. "This isn't the 1940s, you know?"

He smirked. "I know. And trust me, I also know the power I wield in the city, but you'll see."

"What you mean I'll see?" I was confused. "How will I see?"

"You'll just see," he said. "So, Callie, I assume that you're ready for—"

"For what?" I said, interrupting him. Was he going to seduce me? I mean, I wouldn't say no to a kiss. He was hot, and it would make a really great story. I could just imagine calling Imogen and telling her that I made out with a mafia boss. Fuck, I'd even let him go down on me, not that I'd tell him that, but he seemed like he would know what he was doing. And I kind of wanted to be with a guy that knew what he was doing, not that I would tell him that.

"What are you thinking?" he said.

"Why do you keep doing that?"

"Doing what?" he asked me innocently.

"Ask me what I'm thinking."

"Because you have a very expressive face, Callie, and I can tell something dark and naughty crested your brain because your face blushed, and when your face blushes, it's usually because you think it's something, I don't know, naughty."

"I was just thinking that I don't know what you're going to do to me. And I was wondering…" I swallowed hard.

"You were wondering what?" he said.

"If you were going to try and sleep with me or something."

He burst out laughing and shook his head. "My dear, there are two hundred women downstairs begging to have a night with me. I don't need to force you into sleeping with me."

"Okay, well, just checking."

"Unless you're asking me to, of course."

"Of course not," I said, maybe too quickly. I blushed again. I mean, him going down on me wasn't me sleeping with him. Sure, it was more than a kiss on the lips, but it wasn't sex sex. When I had sex, I wanted it to be with someone I loved, someone that loved me. Having an orgasm and a man go down on me, well, I didn't mind if it was just a hot man I met at a random party.

"I think we should get you to your car," he said softly.

I felt surprisingly deflated as he walked over to the door and unlocked it.

"Oh," I said. "You're letting me go?"

"Yes," he said, nodding. "I've gotten the information that I sought. You're just a regular girl who came to help out a friend. I'll let you go now."

"Oh, okay." I followed him out of the room. This

was not how I'd assumed this evening was going to end.

"Unless there was something else you wanted?" he asked.

I shook my head. "No, of course not."

"Okay," he said. "So I'll get you to your driver and then I'd better make an appearance in the ballroom again. My father and all my potential brides will be wondering where I am."

"Oh, yeah, sure. Well, good luck," I said.

"Thank you." He nodded. "I appreciate it."

"I hope you find a really amazing wife that will be the woman of your dreams and you'll be desperately in love. And—"

He burst out laughing then. "You really aren't from my world, are you, Callie?"

"What?" I said, wondering what he was talking about.

"I'm not getting married for love. I don't care if she loves me, and I certainly won't love her. I'm getting married because it's my duty because I will be the leader of the Marchesi family, the most powerful mafia family in the United States. I'm getting married to show that I wield power, that I am in control. It is something I must do." He shrugged. "It's got nothing to do with love. And just remember, little lamb, just because I'm letting you go, it doesn't mean I've forgotten what has occurred tonight. I am a wolf. I am cold, cruel, vindictive, all of the bad things you've heard about me. So before you think about saying anything about tonight to anyone, just remember that."

CHAPTER 13

Antonio

"*Revenge is a kind of wild justice, which the more man's nature runs to, the more ought law to weed it out.*" — Francis Bacon

Callie looked confused as I escorted her through the house toward the exit. I watched as she stepped carefully in her high heels. It was obvious to me that she wasn't someone that normally wore heels that high. She played with her hair and bit down on her lower lip, and I pressed my palm to the small of her back.

"Is everything okay?" I asked in a gruff voice, knowing that confused her even more. I was not known for being someone that showed concern to others.

"Um, I kind of left my duffel bag in one of the

rooms, and I was going to leave it and just say bye to the stuff, but seeing as you already caught me, can I get it please?" she squeaked out. Her bright brown eyes looked at me nervously.

"I don't bite, Callie. Not unless you want me to."

"Okay," she said. "So, that's a yes?"

"Sure. Just show me where it is." I nodded at her, and she let out a wide smile.

"Thank you. You're really not so bad after all, are you?"

I pressed my lips together and shook my head. "Don't be fooled by this little reprieve I've given you. You're very lucky that I'm letting you go, Callie. Don't ever think about trying to sneak onto my property again. The outcome next time will not be as favorable."

All color left her face, and she nodded as her eyes widened. "Okay. Sorry."

She bit down on her lower lip, but I could tell she was nervous, as I wanted her to be. I followed her into the room where she grabbed her duffel bag, slung it over her shoulder, and then hurried back out of the door.

"Okay, we can go to the car now."

"Good," I said. "My father will be wondering where I am."

I let out a small sigh. My father was most probably pissed right now, having people search for me. He knew I'd be back. Of course I wouldn't leave my own party, but he would see this as a sign of disrespect, and we'd have words later. It wasn't that I wanted to show my father disrespect, but some things were more important, and I listened to the beat of my own drum, even though I knew that's not how things were meant to be done.

My phone beeped then, and I pulled it out. Alessandro had texted me.

"You better hurry up, man. Dad is fuming."

I nodded imperceptibly at his text.

"Okay, we are going to have to hurry this up." I grabbed her hand and escorted her down the stairs.

"What's going on?" she said.

"I need to get you out of here. You need to leave."

"Okay. You don't have to come with me."

"I think I do," I said, nodding. "I need to make sure you get into the car and leave."

"Wow," she said. "You really want me gone."

"I mean, it's not like you want to be a part of this, do you?" I asked her, raising an eyebrow. "Are you hoping to become my wife?"

She blushed and shook her head.

"So then are you hoping to sleep with me?"

"No, of course not," she said vehemently.

"Wow. Is it really such a bad proposition?"

"I would never sleep with someone like you. You're a brute," she said.

I chuckled then. "That's a little bit closer to the truth." I nodded.

We exited the front door. I nodded at the soldiers and headed toward the front where all the cars were parked.

"Where are you?"

She looked around and made a face. "Um, this is going to sound really bad, but I'm not quite sure."

"What do you mean, you're not quite sure?"

"I know I was in a limo, but there are a lot of limos here."

"What was your driver's name?" I asked her, stifling a sigh.

"I can't remember." She shook her head. "I'm horrible with names." She sighed. "I used to do this trick where I would repeat the name several times in conversation right after I learned it, but we didn't get to have a conversation because he had the window up and there was no way to speak to him. Well, I guess I could have just spoken into the speaker in the darkness, but that would've been weird and..." She bit down on her lower lip. "Sorry."

"It's fine." I looked around. "And he knows you as Valentina or Callie?"

She shrugged. "I don't know."

This was absolutely ridiculous. Was this girl a complete idiot? She'd gotten into a limo with a driver she didn't know to go to a party she knew nothing about for someone who didn't even seem to be her friend and then faked her way into a party for the mafia. I was a mafia underboss, and even I wouldn't recommend a civilian do that.

I stepped forward and held my hand up and then whistled. The drivers, well, at least, most of them, headed toward me once they recognized who I was.

"Does anyone recognize this girl behind me? She goes by Valentina, AKA Callie."

A short man shuffled forward, a black cap on his head. "She is with me." He nodded. He looked slightly nervous. "Is everything okay?"

"She's not feeling well," I said softly. "She needs to go home, and right home."

"Yes, sir." He nodded.

I looked back at Callie, who was staring at me with mesmerized eyes. I could tell she wasn't sure what to think of me, and that was fine by me.

"Go home, little lamb," I said, shaking my head at her. "And maybe think before you take action next time."

"Yes, sir," she said, nodding, and I chuckled.

"I'm not that much older than you. You can call me…"

"The Wolf?" she said, slight attitude in her voice.

So, the spunk was back.

"If you want to call me The Wolf." I shrugged. "I also go by Antonio."

"I don't know you like that, Mr. Marchesi."

I laughed then. She really was something else.

"Well, you have a good evening, Callie. Just remember…"

"What?" she said.

"You're never going to be smarter than Antonio The Wolf Marchesi." And with that, I left her and headed back toward the house. I knew I had to get back into the ballroom before my father absolutely flipped a switch.

I headed inside, and I could feel her eyes on me, but I didn't turn around. I didn't stop to make sure she got in the car. I didn't give her a wave. She had been dismissed. She had to know that, when she was dealing with me, I wasn't a soft, caring man. I was cold. I was cruel. Some people even called me pompous, vindictive, mean. I didn't mind any of those adjectives. I wasn't here to make friends.

"There you are, Antonio. Your father's been looking for you." Vinny spoke in hushed tones. I nodded as I walked into the room.

Two hundred women's faces turned to me, along with several fathers and uncles who were wondering what was going on. I walked up to my father, who was standing in the middle. His face was an ugly, contorted red.

"I've been looking for you, Antonio."

"I had some business to take care of," I said, and he frowned. "Continue, Papa."

"Well, ladies and gentlemen, the moment you have all been waiting for," he said loudly into the microphone. "I present to you my son, the under-boss of the Marchesi family, Antonio."

The room burst into applause as if I'd just won the Nobel Peace Prize or something, and I nodded my head slightly. I gave a wan smile as I looked around the room; eager eyes stared back at me. Many women were batting their eyelashes and twirling their hair, and several were pushing forward their bosoms, hoping I'd like what I saw.

I stepped forward and grabbed the microphone.

"My apologies to everyone for the wait. I had some business to take care of. As most of you under-stand, the business always comes first." I looked around the room, waiting for the applause and slight laughter I knew they owed me. I didn't have to wait long.

"As we know, I am in need of a wife, someone who will be a good match, someone who will become the wife of the leader of the Marchesi family. My father obviously is still the don, but one day I will assume power, and once I do, we will become the largest mafia syndicates in the world, larger than the Bratva, larger than the Triads, larger than the Irish," I said, and everyone started chanting, "Marchesi! Marchesi! Marchesi!"

I could see that my father wasn't pleased because my words were a slight to him. We were the largest family in New York, and most probably in the United States, but the Bratva, who were the Russian mobsters, were growing in size exponentially, and they were crueler, meaner than us. They were taking over, and I would not let that stand.

"I am seeking a wife that understands that being married to a man like me comes with certain challenges, but also certain pleasures."

A slight tickle of laughter across the room. I could see a couple of women blushing and some looking excited. My prowess in the bedroom was well known in the community. I was known as a man that gave pleasure before he received, but I almost certainly received as well.

"So, let the party commence. I will make the rounds and dance, my dears. Let us have fun."

I nodded at Sylvio, who was standing in the corner next to the small five-piece brass band that was waiting to play music, and he started leading the band into music.

"What was going on, Antonio?" my father said in hushed tones as he approached me.

"As I said, Father, business."

"What business?"

"It doesn't matter now. It's been settled. Let's not fight here in front of our guests."

He nodded and turned toward Tommaso, his consigliere. I tried not to sigh as I saw Serena standing there.

"Oh, hello again, Antonio," she said, walking over to me, pressing her hand against my arm. "I wanted you to know that, as my father is the consigliere for the Marchesi family, I am in a very—"

"Not now," I said, "Serena." I shook my head and walked toward the other side of the room.

A slightly older woman by the name of Graziella hurried over to me. Her dark eyes roved up and down my body.

"You're very handsome," she said in her Italian accent. She was part of a Sicilian family that was desperate to make connections with us in the States.

"Thank you," I said, nodding.

She was gorgeous with her long, dark hair and dark eyes. She wore a black dress that accentuated every curve.

"You'd like to go to a room?" she said, smiling, running her finger across her lips and then sucking on it. "There are many things I can do to show you I would make a very good wife."

"Oh, really?" I said huskily. "And what would those things be?"

"Well," she said, "I could make you very happy indeed."

She pushed two fingers into her mouth now and sucked, and I just smiled. She reached forward and rubbed the front of my pants. I was still semi-hard from my moments with Callie, and she smiled to herself, thinking that largeness was for her.

"I see you like it already."

I grabbed her hands and squeezed, not too

tightly, but with enough pressure to let her know I wasn't interested. I removed her hands from my crotch and nodded. "I have to go. But thank you for the offer. I'm sure my father would be more than excited to take you up on it."

Her eyes widened in shock as she gasped, and I headed out of the room. I'd said my piece. For now, I was done. It had been a long evening, and while I knew I was being rude, there was not one woman in this room I wanted to marry.

CHAPTER 14

Callie

"You can't blame gravity for falling in love." — Albert Einstein

The sun was shining through the bedroom window as I sat at my desk. I had homework to do, but I wasn't able to concentrate. The activities of Saturday night still weighed on my mind, and I felt frustrated because I hadn't been able to speak to Valentina about what had gone down. She hadn't been back to the room since I had arrived back in the limo.

I jumped up and ran my fingers through my hair. I knew I wasn't going to be able to concentrate on calculus right now. I was about to head out to grab something to eat from the local bodega on the corner when my phone started ringing.

I grabbed it quickly. It was Imogen. "Hey, hey, what's going on?" she asked, sounding pepped up and happy.

"Not much. What are you doing?" I knew my voice was low-key, but I just wasn't able to fake a smile or happiness right now.

"Oh my gosh. I had the absolute most amazing weekend. I went to this... Well, you can't judge me. Okay?"

"Where did you go?" I asked her, knowing that her weekend couldn't even have come close to mine.

"I went to this party and guess what?"

"I don't know. What?" I asked.

"No, you have to guess Callie, and then I'll tell you."

"I don't know. It was a party for a mafia boss," I said facetiously.

"No, of course not. How would I wind up at a party for a mafia boss?"

"Don't ask," I mumbled under my breath.

"It was a party for these personal assistants to a couple of A-list stars, and they took us to you will never guess whose house."

"I don't know. The mafia boss's house?"

"What are you talking about? Did you watch *The Godfather* or something and now you're obsessed with the mafia?"

"Nope. That's not what happened."

"Hey," she said suddenly, her voice changing. "Is everything okay, Callie?"

"No, it's not okay. I've been calling you and calling you and texting you because I had the most fucked-up and crazy night, and you didn't call me back, and now you've called me back and all you're going on about is your amazing weekend, and you haven't asked me why I called you ten times."

"Sorry, girl. My battery was dead. I didn't even know you called me ten times."

"Well, that's even worse. What if something would've happened?"

"What if something would've happened where? In your dorm room? Did something happen at school that I don't know about?"

"No. Valentina, my roommate, asked me to go to a party for her, and it ended up being a party for a mafia boss who was looking for a wife, and he found out I was lying and wasn't Valentina, and I thought he was going to kill me or rape me or, I don't know, do something. But instead, he put me in my car and sent me packing."

I let out a huge breath. It was finally all out.

"Callie, are you high?" Imogen asked, sounding shocked. "Do you need me to call your dad to get you to go to the hospital? What are you on?"

"I'm not on anything, Imogen."

There was silence on the phone.

"So what you just said was true?"

"Yes, it was."

"You went to a party for a fucking mafia boss? Are you kidding me right now? That is so fucking awesome," Imogen said, sounding excited for me, and I burst out laughing.

"Imogen, it's not awesome. It's scary. I was freaking scared out of my mind."

"Dude, when will you ever do anything like that again?" she said. "And did he look scary? Was he like an Al Capone sort of mobster?"

"You've watched way too many movies, Imogen."

"What? Did he look like Joe Pesci or closer to Robert DeNiro? Or did he have that Pacino look? Or did he look like Marlon Brando? Do you have a problem with me?" she said, her voice lowering.

I started laughing then. "Imogen, this is not funny, but I love you. Thank you for making me feel lighter about the situation."

"Shit, so you were scared?"

"Girl, I was scared, and the guy, he was young. He wasn't some old fart. He was in his twenties, and he was really good looking and..."

"Wow, like he was hot?"

"I mean, I don't know that I would say hot," I lied. I didn't want Imogen to think I was interested in him. I certainly didn't want her to know that I had dreamed about him the last two nights and that his lips had been places they shouldn't have been because, well, it kind of embarrassed me.

"So you went to a party for a hot mafia boss, and what do you mean he was trying to get married? What the fuck? Is he like Prince Charming or something?"

"Girl, I didn't really understand what was going on, but supposedly all these women from other mafia families were there because he's looking for a wife. I don't know why or what was going on, but it was really weird, and it was this mansion in the country, and everyone was really dressed up and looked super rich, and it was just crazy."

"Why did you think he was going to kill you?"

"I mean, I didn't actually think he was going to kill me kill me. I didn't get that vibe from him, but he was carrying a gun. In fact, all of the men were carrying guns, and they were scary. Like scary, scary. Scarier than the cops."

"Cops aren't scary," she said. "Cops are fucking hot."

"I mean, most cops are fucking hot, but have you ever seen that one cop, like when you're walking down the street after the bar and he gives you that look like you better not be fucking drunk and walking home or about to drive?"

She started giggly. "No, Callie, I've never seen that cop, but I might like to."

"What do you mean you might like to?"

"Girl, he can dominate me anytime."

I groaned. "Really, Imogen?"

"What? I'm telling you, there is a difference being with a guy who is passive as opposed to dominant."

"I wouldn't know," I said. "I'm still a virgin, thank you very much."

"I know, and I totally respect you for that. Callie, you're amazing. You will be a virgin when you get married. You're saving yourself for the right man."

"I'm not actually saving myself for the right man," I burst out. "And I don't want to be a virgin when I get married. I just haven't met a guy that does it for me enough that I would want to hook up with him in that way."

"I know," she said. "Well, anyway, let me continue about my weekend because…"

My phone started beeping then. "Hold on," I said as I looked at the screen. Gia's name showed up. "Hey, let me call you back. I have to take this."

"But I didn't even get to—"

"Speak to you later, Imogen," I said quickly and switched over the phone line. "Hi, Gia?"

"Hey, Callie. How's it going?" she said softly.

"Not bad. I didn't expect to hear from you."

I was surprised to hear from her. She had been lovely at the party, and I did want to stay in contact, but when I hadn't heard from her the next day, I thought I wouldn't hear from her.

"I wanted to make sure you got home okay," she said, "and didn't break an arm climbing down the tree or anything."

"Yeah, I got home fine. Thank you." I didn't really know what to say. "Was everything fun at the party? Did Antonio choose his wife?"

"Girl, the party was crazy. His dad was pissed. He ended up leaving the party after about fifteen minutes, and no one saw him again."

"Oh, wow. So did he go with someone?"

Jealous thoughts passed through my brain. Maybe he just grabbed someone and fucked her in a room or something.

"I don't know. I don't think so." She shrugged. "Everyone was accounted for, and Serena was fucking pissed."

"Who's Serena?" I asked curiously.

"Serena is someone that hooked up with him. Her dad is Tommasso. He's a consigliere for the family."

"I don't really know what that means." I laughed.

"Oh, well, basically he's the intermediary between Roberto, who's the don of the family, and Antonio, who's the underboss. Basically, he's not meant to take sides. He deals with lawyery issues and accounting issues and running of the business. If there's like issues with other members of the family, he's meant to have an unbiased view, but he totally doesn't."

"Oh?" I asked.

"Oh, he is literally hanging on Roberto's ass

cheeks." She laughed. "Which Antonio knows, so that he would never marry Serena or her sisters."

"Oh, okay. But they used to date?"

"I don't know if you could say Antonio dates as opposed to fucks," she said. "He's not a guy I would recommend to any of my girlfriends."

"Oh wow."

"Yeah, I guess he just wasn't brought up that way. He's not into romance or doing sweet things. You know?"

"You know a lot about him."

"Remember, I used to be best friends with Alessandro. I saw a lot of things growing up."

"Oh yeah, I forgot that."

"I mean, they're both nice enough guys at their core, but I think their mother's death affected them."

"Oh, I hadn't realized that their mother was dead. What happened?"

"She died in a car crash," she said softly. "I don't think they ever got over it. I'm pretty sure they think Roberto was the one responsible."

And then suddenly I remembered I'd heard this before. "Oh yeah. That's horrible," I said.

"But yeah, I just wanted to see if you wanted to catch up for lunch or something later this week."

"That would be great. I'd love to."

"Awesome. Well, I better go now. I've got some studying to do. Chem final coming up."

"Oh, that sucks," I said softly. "Good luck."

"Thanks, Callie, and I'm glad you made it home safely."

"Me too," I said. "Thanks."

We hung up the phone, and I walked back over to my desk. I picked up my pen and twirled it in my fingers, thoughtfully wondering about what had happened at the party after I'd left. Where had Antonio gone? Had he gone to a room with Serena or someone else? Or was he pissed off that he had to get married? Was he hoping that he'd find a true love?

Immediately, I started laughing. Antonio was not the sort of man that was looking for love. I didn't know him well, but even that much was evident to me. I buried my face in my hands and rubbed my forehead. I was annoyed that I was still thinking about him. It had been quite obvious to me that he wasn't interested. The way he sent me packing, he hadn't cared about me. He hadn't been intrigued by the girl who'd shown up to the party for her room-mate. He'd gotten the truth, been satisfied that I wasn't holding anything back, and then sent me on my way.

When he'd left, he hadn't even looked back or waved or made sure I got into the car. I'd been dismissed and forgotten quite easily. It hurt my feel-ings slightly, though I knew it was for the best. I mean, what would I have wanted to happen? Would I have wanted him to take me to his bedroom and try to seduce me? Would I have wanted him to press his warm, firm, juicy lips against mine and give me the first real kiss of my life? I didn't know.

I knew that the idea of it didn't scare me no matter what I said. I knew that the possibility of it gave me a slight thrill. I jumped up and sighed. I was not going to be able to concentrate. I wasn't really hungry, either. I decided I'd walk to the library and get some fresh air. Maybe that would help.

CHAPTER 15

Antonio

"Revenge is barren of itself; itself is the dreadful food it feeds on; its delight is murder, and its satiety, despair." — Friedrich Schiller

"Mama, your meatballs, they taste juicy." My papa held his pinkies up into the air as he grabbed a spoon to try and steal some of the sauce that my nonna had been working on all morning.

"Roberto, put that spoon away," she snapped at him, hitting him on the shoulder.

"But Mama, I just want to taste the sauce." My father squinted his nose as he tried to dip the spoon into the pot.

"I said no, Roberto."

"Fine. Fine. I just buy all the ingredients for the sauce and the meatballs, and I cannot taste."

My nana put his spoon into the sauce, held it up, and tasted it. "It needs a little bit more thyme. Antonio, come." I walked over to her dutifully. "Taste the sauce."

My father looked at me with disdain in his eyes. It annoyed him that his mother spoiled me so.

"Sorry, Papa, when you don't beg, you are given freely."

He rolled his eyes and huffed out of the room to the living room. My father and I only ever let down our guard when we are at my grandmother's house. When I was younger, I used to think that my grandmother didn't know that my dad was part of the mafia, that we led a different life when we weren't here. But now that I'd grown older, I came to realize that it was a separate life. She fully understood and was even proud of her son and proud of her grandsons. She knew what we did, and she didn't judge us, but for her, all that mattered was feeding us and having us by her side every Sunday.

"So, Antonio, I hear you are getting married," she said, looking into my brown eyes. Her blue ones were warm and happy.

"Not yet, Nonna," I said, laughing.

"But I want you to marry a nice Italian girl, preferably from Sicilia."

"I don't meet many women from Sicilia, Nonna."

"Yes, but I have some friends, and I tell you my one friend's granddaughter, she is…" she paused.

"Well, I don't like to say this. She's a little bit plump, but she make good wife. She cook, she clean. She can do everything, and she knows our ways. Her grandfather consiglieri in Sicilia and her father underboss. Her father died from gunfight with the Bratva, but she know our world. I introduce you. Si?"

"No, Nonna." I shook my head. "That's okay. I already have far too many women."

"But that is the problem. When you have many, you don't want one. And if you can't choose one, your nonna will help you pick. You know I make good match for you, Antonio."

"Why don't you ask Alessandro?" I said softly, and Nonna rolled her eyes.

"Alessandro, he be the death of me. He's not serious. He not serious enough for wife. He not serious enough for life."

"Did I hear my name?" Alessandro's humor-filled voice bounded into the room ahead of him. He chuckled slightly as he looked over at me and Nonna. "Stealing meatballs from underneath me, Antonio?"

"Would I do that, bro?"

"Yeah, you've done it all your life." He chuckled, and I laughed as he walked over and gave Nonna two big kisses on the cheek.

She blustered and smiled at him happily. Even though Alessandro was, as she said, not as serious, he was definitely her favorite. I knew she loved me and treated me like a king, especially above my father. But she had a soft spot for Alessandro. Maybe it was because he was just devastatingly handsome and reminded her of her late husband. Maybe it was because he spent time with her taking her shopping and playing cards and doing all the things that my father and I were just too busy to do.

"Nonna, did you make cannoli?" he asked.

"No cannoli for you," she said.

Alessandro and I looked at each other and shook our heads.

"But, Nonna, you know we love your cannoli," I said.

"Did you at least make tiramisu?" Alessandro asked her.

"No tiramisu. No cannoli, no..." She giggled. "Okay. I cannot lie, but cannoli not to be eaten until after spaghetti and meatballs, and after we have some lasagna and after..."

"Nonna, lasagna and spaghetti and meatballs?"

"And veal parmigiana." She smiled. "And eggplant parmigiana and garlic bread and salad. And I also have some limoncello that your cousin Silverio just brought back from Italia. He was in Roma and Florencia. I say to him, 'Why you not going visit your family in Sicilia?' And he say, 'Nonna, I cannot go to Sicilia if I'm going to Roma and Florencia.' And I said, 'Why you cannot go to Sicilia? You have family there and your family want to see you.' And he say..." She paused, and I pressed my lips together.

"Nonna, I'm going to take this opportunity to just make a phone call. I'll be right back." I smiled at Alessandro. "Will you listen to Nonna for me? I have some work to do."

He rolled his eyes at me. "You've always got work to do."

I headed out of the kitchen chuckling as I pulled out my phone. I saw that I did have some messages from Jimmy, and I wanted to figure out what was going on.

"So, Antonio, we need to talk," my father said as he sat in his father's armchair and smoked on his cigar.

It was funny how my father liked to think he ruled the roost yet, as soon as my nonna would walk out of the kitchen into the living room, he would jump up. No one sat in Nono's chair. Not even my dad.

"What is it, Dad? I have got some business to take care of. Jimmy just messaged me."

"What happened at the party cannot happen again," he said, shaking his head. "You embarrassed me. You embarrassed the Marchesi name. You made families feel like we were disrespecting them. People came from far and wide. They send their daughters, and yet you not spend time with many of them."

"Dad, I was overwhelmed. They were just..."

"You need to find a wife, Antonio. You know I will not be don forever, and I cannot pass on until you are married."

I pressed my lips together. I wasn't sure why my father was so insistent on me getting married. Maybe it was because he knew how much I would hate it. Or maybe it was because he wanted the leader of the familia to be a family man, at least in people's eyes.

Everyone talked about my dad, how all three of his wives had passed away, how he didn't respect any of them. I'd heard rumors that he beat and smacked around every single one of them.

I bit down on my lower lip. Sometimes I wondered if that was why my mom had done it, why she found another man. Sometimes I wanted to hate her because if she hadn't been cheating on my dad, then she wouldn't have been in the car and she wouldn't have crashed. She wouldn't have died, and she wouldn't have left me and Alessandro to fend for ourselves against him, a brute of a monster.

My father and I had history, and while I respected his power, I didn't respect who he was. Not just because of what he'd done to my mother or how he treated people, but what he'd done to Alessandro and me. What he'd done to us when we were boys. How he tried to make us men without caring how much physical and mental and emotional pain he put us through.

Now that he was older, he liked to say that he made us who we were. That we wouldn't be strong, we wouldn't be cold, and we wouldn't be calculating without his influence. And while I believe that to be somewhat true, that didn't mean I forgave him for everything that he'd done. It didn't mean that I could forget the nights when his belt had hit my back for insolence or for being weak. I would never forget those moments, those days.

He was on my list, a short list I had of people I wanted to exact revenge upon at some point in my life. But he wasn't first nor even second. He'd have his moment, though, and when I was done with him, he would regret the way he treated me, Alessandro, and my mother. For now, I had to at least partially pretend I respected what he had to say.

"I will arrange some dates within the next week with some of the women I find most suitable," I said. I held up my hand. "I'm going outside. I'm going to take this call with Jimmy."

"Fine," he said, looking pissed off. "I need to call Tommasso anyway. He wants to know if Serena is on your short list."

I stared at my father. He wasn't asking me a question. He was telling me Serena was to be on the short list.

I pressed my lips together, and he shrugged. "Look, Antonio, as I said before, I don't care who you fucking marry. It can be Serena, it can be V, it can be the other sister. I can't even remember her fucking name. But it has to be someone from our world. It has to be someone that understands the duties that come from being married to the leader of the Marchesi Familia. You get it?"

"Yes, Papa." I nodded.

I exited Nonna's back door and walked into the yard and called Jimmy.

"Hey, boss. What's happening?"

"Not much. I saw your text. What's going on?"

"We've got some issues. Florence on Fifth."

"What, again?"

"Yeah," he said. "And that's not all."

"Let me guess. Melvin's Pizzeria."

"Yeah, how'd you know?"

"We are pretty sure we caught some dirty money when we were counting last week."

"Yeah. Okay. But we've also got a problem elsewhere, boss."

"Oh?"

"That little place in the Village."

"The bar?" I asked.

We'd recently purchased a cute little bar in the Village. It was one of our legitimate businesses, but of course we had men from the family helping to run it. You had to when you were in the mafia. We were all in it together.

"I think you're going to have to come down, boss. We're going to have to hire some new people. Some people on the outside. They don't know shit about how to run a bar, especially one like this. Some chick asked for a bunch of different cocktails yesterday, and Lucio, he just poured beers for all of them. We've already started getting some bad reviews."

I sighed. "Okay, put an ad in the paper."

"Sounds good." He nodded. "We've got one going in for the pizzeria this week as well."

I smiled to myself. "I know."

"Okay, well, I'll speak to you later, boss?"

"Sounds good," I said and hung up.

Everything was going according to plan. I'd have to give Vee a call later. Let her know what to do.

CHAPTER 16

Callie

"And now here is my secret, a very simple secret; it is only with the heart that one can see rightly, what is essential is invisible to the eye." — Antoine de Saint Exupery

"Callie, so good to see you." Gia stood up from her seat and gave me a quick hug. "You look different today."

I burst out laughing, then. I knew exactly what she meant by different. She meant I didn't look glamorous or pretty. I just looked normal in my oversize NYU sweater, black leggings. My hair was up in a messy bun, and I was wearing my glasses.

"And you look stunning."

"Well, I did go to the spa this morning," she said, shrugging. "I wanted a me day."

"That sounds really nice," I said.

"You should come with me next time. I go to this amazing place on the Upper West Side. I get a facial, a full-body massage. Then I lounge around in the sauna for a little bit, have a swim, and then sometimes I also have a scrub."

"Wow, that sounds really cool."

"And it's a really great price."

"Oh yeah?" I asked hopefully.

I'd never been to a spa before. It never really crossed my mind to go to one, and I also never thought I could afford one, but if it was a really great price, maybe it was affordable.

"Like what? Twenty dollars?" I asked, and Gia made a face.

"Are you being serious?"

"Oh, I guess that's a little bit low." I laughed. "Fifty dollars?"

"Fifty dollars for a spa with a massage, and a facial and everything I just listed?" She shook her head. "No, it was five hundred ninety-five dollars on sale from seven hundred ninety-five dollars, which is an amazing deal. Two hundred dollars off."

My jaw dropped. That was a lot of money to pretty much everyone I thought. She was a college student just like me. How on earth did she think $595 was not a lot of money?

"Oh, I'm sorry," she said, lightly touching my hand and wrinkling her nose. "I didn't think to ask if you were well off or not." She sighed. "It's a problem

I have. I just assume everyone has money because in the mafia world we normally do." She made a face. "Which I mean doesn't mean anything. It's not like we're the Bill Gates of crime or whatever." She shrugged and then laughed. "Anyway, I don't know what I'm saying, but I guess that's a lot of money, huh?"

"Yeah, it kind of is." I nodded. "In fact, I'm definitely not going to be able to go. In fact, I wouldn't have been able to go if it was fifty dollars."

"You wouldn't have been able to go if it was fifty dollars?" she asked.

"No. My dad is not doing well financially, and I am on scholarship at NYU, but my dad was paying for my accommodation and for living expenses and food, and he can't afford to do that right now. So I'm actually going to be getting a job." I sighed. "Sucks."

"Oh, I'm sorry to hear that. What does your dad do again?"

"Well, he used to be a reporter, and then he worked at the mayor's office. That's how I met my best friend Imogen."

"Oh, cool. Does she live in the city as well?"

"She used to. She's in Berkeley now in California. She moved for uni. She goes to Cal Berkeley."

"Oh, cool." She nodded. "So she's a bear."

"Yeah, I guess she is. Anyway, he no longer works there. He was doing other odd jobs, and he had a piece of land, well, a property that he rented, but I don't really understand what's going on. But the city is saying that it's not zoned for commercial use, and he was renting it to someone who was using it for their business." I shrugged. "I don't know. It sucks."

"Can't he speak to his contacts at the mayor's office?" she asked.

I shook my head. "So when he worked at the mayor's office, it was a different mayor." I laughed. "And the staff have all changed. So he doesn't have any contacts there anymore. He kind of lost all interest in work and life when my mom died, and well, we've sort of been struggling for a long time. But now I need to help out as best as I can."

"Aww, I'm sorry," she said. "That sounds rough."

"Yeah, just a little bit."

"Maybe you should marry Antonio after all. He's made of money." I stared at her then, and she burst out laughing. "Okay, maybe it was too soon for that joke."

"Just a little soon," I said, laughing. "So you really know his family well, huh?"

"Yeah. The Marchesi family in the mafia world is like, I don't know, the Brad Pitt and George Clooney of Hollywood. Everyone knows them."

"Wow. That's crazy."

"And he's not even don yet," she said. "But I heard his father's on the way out soon, and he will be don, and when he's don, oh boy. A lot of people better watch out."

"What do you mean?"

She leaned forward. "I really shouldn't be gossiping about mafia stuff to someone that's not in this world, but I trust you."

"You do?"

"Yeah. Even though I shouldn't." She laughed. "Seeing as you pretended to be someone else at a party. But…"

"It was because my roommate told me she wanted to be with her boyfriend Maksim."

"Who was your roommate again?"

"Her name's Valentina," I said quickly.

"Oh yeah, Valentina, Serena's sister."

"Oh, I didn't know she had any sisters."

"I know Valentina. Really gorgeous. Really full of herself. Has all the men circling?" she asked me, and I nodded.

I thought it was quite ironic that Gia was describing Valentina as really beautiful with all the men circling because Gia was most probably even more beautiful than Valentina, though she certainly didn't have the attitude like Valentina.

"Everyone knows Valentina, and I don't know why she told you to go because Antonio would not have been interested in her."

"Oh, why is that?" I asked. "Who wouldn't be interested in Valentina?"

"Because he fucked her sister and their dad Tommasso is the consiglieri that I was telling you about, and everyone knows Antonio hates Tommasso. In fact," she leaned forward and whispered in my ear, "he thinks Tommasso is the reason why his mother is dead."

My jaw dropped. "So I know you mentioned before that he thought his dad had her killed, but..."

"Oh, Roberto doesn't do anything himself. He tells Tommasso, which technically shouldn't be what happens. Normally the boss would tell the underboss and the underboss makes it happen. But Roberto and Tommasso are like this." She held her fingers together. "Anything Roberto wants done, Tommasso will do, and anything Tommasso wants, Roberto will do. I guess aside from this one thing." She leaned back and smiled a wicked little smile on her face.

"Oh, what's that?"

"Tommasso wants Serena to be the mafia boss's wife, but there's no way that Roberto's going to get Antonio to agree to marry Serena. We all know it, and when that happens, all hell is going to break loose."

"Oh, why is that?"

"Because then Tommasso will have to see Antonio's fucking his daughter as disrespect, which technically it already is, but I think he figured if they get married it's okay." She leaned back. "We still have a slightly archaic system. When Antonio gets married, they'll have to parade the sheets the morning after the wedding."

"Parade the sheets? What do you mean?"

"So a mafia bride, especially the boss's wife, has to be pure and innocent. And so he has to prove to the world that he is in control and has de-flowered her. So the sheets should be bloody. They're paraded in front of all the families to see, to say and show that he took her virtue."

"Oh my gosh. That is archaic."

"I told you." She nodded. "I mean it's absolutely ridiculous. But someone like Antonio, he will definitely want to prove that, and well, let's be real. Serena's already fucked him, and she didn't keep it secret. She basically let everyone she knows how big he was and let's just say he's working with a salami." She bit down on her lower lip. "Though it kind of freaks me out to think that because he's kind of like a brother to me, though he's not."

"So you wouldn't marry him?" I asked, questioning her again. She certainly was going on and on about Antonio as if she were interested.

"Oh no." She made a face. "I would never want to be a part of the Marchesi family. No, thank you. It's bad enough that I spent so many of my formative years with Alessandro. No, thank you." She took a sip of her water and then jumped up. "Come on, let's get some coffees and some pastries. My treat, by the way."

"Oh no, you don't have to do that," I said quickly.

"No, you just told me how broke you are, and I have plenty of money." She shrugged. "And I'm not trying to show off, even though I know that sounded incredibly douchy. I'm not like that. I just want to treat you. I am so glad that we met and can be friends."

"Thanks, Gia," I said gratefully. "I'm glad I met you, too. Even if it was because I was gate-crashing a mafia boss's party, which I still can't believe. I mean, I knew the mafia existed back in the day. I didn't even know it was still a thing."

"Oh, it's definitely still a thing, and the turf war is crazier than ever right now. In fact, that's why Antonio has to show he's strong." She shrugged.

"Why? What do you mean?"

"I don't know all the ins and outs of it. It's still a pretty sexist system where only men are at the top and only men are meant to be in the know. But us women, we hear things and we talk."

"Oh, okay."

Even though I wasn't a part of the world and didn't really understand half the things she was talking about, I wanted to know more information, if only because it made me feel closer to Antonio in a weird sort of way. And I didn't even want to question why I wanted to feel close to Antonio and to understand his world. I mean, it wasn't even like I'd ever see him again.

I don't even know what part of upstate New York his mansion had been in. I knew he spent time in Manhattan as well, but it was a big city, and we were unlikely to navigate the same circles. As much as I wouldn't mind seeing him again and bantering back and forth, I knew that wasn't going to happen. He'd be relegated to my dreams and fantasies, and most probably that was better because in my dreams and fantasies, I could control everything. He wouldn't be mean. He wouldn't be cold. He wouldn't threaten my life, and he certainly wouldn't play with the gun around his waist.

"Hey, you okay there, Callie?" Gia asked me as we headed toward the front of the coffee shop.

"Yeah, sorry. I was just daydreaming and thinking."

"It's okay. You must have been so overwhelmed at that party. I just can't even imagine what you were thinking."

"I was freaking out." I nodded. "Totally and utterly freaking out. But it was a bit of an adventure," I admitted. "And I've kind of wanted an adventure in my life."

"Maybe that was a little bit too much of an adventure," she said. "Oh my gosh, I just had a great idea," she said quickly. "Do you want to go to yoga with me?"

"I'm not really that good at yoga, and I don't know that I can afford it," I said. "I'm sorry."

"No, no, no, it's fine. My uncle owns the studio, so I can get you in for free, and it will be so much fun. I actually just started this acroyoga class and there are lots of cute guys. I think you'd love it."

"Acroyoga, huh?" I hadn't even heard of it before. "I mean, I guess I could try sometime. Sounds like it would be fun."

"It will be so much fun." She linked palms with me. "Oh, I am so happy we met Callie. You are the best civilian girlfriend a girl like me could ask for."

"You don't have many friends?" I asked her. "In the mafia?"

She burst out laughing, then. "Oh, not really. In our world, it's a lot based on hierarchy. So the higher up you are, the less friends you have." She shrugged. "I didn't mind it. It helped me to concentrate on studying, and I got into Columbia and I was able to go, which is amazing. But I haven't really bonded with anyone at Columbia, and well, it's been a little lonesome, but now we've met and we can be friends."

"Yeah," I said, wondering what her story was.

For as nice as Gia was, she wasn't particularly open about anything. I didn't really know who she was as a person, aside from outwardly friendly. I wanted to get to know her better. I wanted to get to know who she was to further the friendship even more.

CHAPTER 17

Antonio

"Revenge is private and personal, and so readily gets out of hand." — Ernest Lucas

"Welcome to Lupo's," the cute blond hostess greeted me. "Do you have a reservation, sir?" The question made me smirk. This girl obviously had no idea who she was talking to. The manager, Lucio, hurried to the front of the bar.

"Antonio, I didn't know you were coming in today." He nudged the blonde out of the way. "This is Birgette. She's new."

"I figured." I nodded as I looked around the half-empty bar. "How's business?" I asked casually. Lucio was new to the role, and I wasn't yet sure if I trusted him.

"Slow, but things are picking up." He grabbed a

menu and handed it to me. "We've added some signature food items like you suggested. Tuna tartare and calamari with an aioli sauce."

"I suggested that?" I didn't like words being put into my mouth. "I think I suggested a meatball, derivative of my nonna's, that we could call Nonna's meatball."

"Well, yeah, but we don't have her recipe and I thought…" His voice trailed off as I was walked away from him and into the bar. I was done listening to him. He could talk to Alessandro if he really needed to hear himself talking.

The bar top was dusty and felt of grease, and I could smell rotting meat as I walked into the kitchen. I could feel my blood pressure rising as the head chef and one of the waitresses jumped apart, guilty expressions on their faces.

"Am I paying you to fuck around on the job?" I grabbed a butcher's knife and stared at the tip.

"No, sir." The chef practically pushed the girl to her feet as he hurried over to his station. "I was just—"

"Fucking around," I finished his sentence for him. "Why does it smell like a rotting carcass in here? Is the freezer out?"

"Oh, it's not the meat," he said quickly, and he looked away.

"Then what the—" I stopped as he let out a large grumbling sound that was quickly followed by the smell of ammonia. "What the fuck is in your stom-ach?" I rubbed my nose and pushed past him. "You stink."

I walked back to the front of the bar, where Lucio was still babbling to Alessandro about his idea for pastrami fries. Bloody idiot.

"They're all fired." I placed my hand on Lucio's shoulder and squeezed. "Do you hear me?" I stared into his frightened eyes and felt a sense of satisfac-tion. "I didn't buy this place for it to be a literal shit-show. You've got a week. Hire some new people. Good people. No family members for now unless they're suited. I put a lot of money into this place, Lucio."

"Yes, boss." He nodded and gulped.

"You know how much money?" I continued. "Ten million dollars." I paused to let the figure sink into his thick brain. "You know how much shit you got to clean up if you cost me my ten million?"

"No, boss." His face was a pale white now. He knew that the only shit he'd be cleaning up was his own if he didn't get his act together.

"This place is a shitshow. You hire some people with experience. You get this bar on the fucking map. You said you could do this right?"

"I'm not sure, I…" His voice trailed off as I showed him the butcher knife still in my hand. "I got this, boss."

"Good." I looked over at Alessandro, who was

grinning at the sight before him. He loved to see me put the fear of God into our men. "Let's go."

"Where we going?" he asked, surprised we were leaving so quickly.

"Let's hit up a strip club." I spoke nonchalantly as we left the bar. "I bet it's been a minute since you got your dick rubbed."

"Since when have you cared when I got any action?" He stared at me quizzically as we made our way into the busy street. Tourists roamed up and down, looking for cute little bistros and boutiques, not paying attention to us as they talked excitedly to each other.

"I don't, but I figured we could talk."

"About the gatecrasher..." He winked at me. "Callie?"

"No." I shook my head. There was nothing left to say about her just yet. "About you and Gia."

"What about us?" He frowned and pulled out his phone. "I think Carmine's is open now. They got some new girls in. Jimmy told me there's a girl from Brazil that can—"

"I don't give a shit about any girls from Brazil. Why did your friendship with Gia end?"

"She's too immature." He shrugged. "I don't know."

"She's too immature?" I raised an eyebrow, and then I had an idea. "I'm thinking I'll propose to her, get Dad off my back, and move on with my life."

"Gia?" He cocked his head to the side and considered my face lazily. It was almost an Oscar-worthy performance, if not for the throbbing vein in his forehead and the dark look in his eyes.

"You wouldn't care, right? You never fucked or anything?"

"No, we didn't fuck." He was pissed now, angry even. Something was definitely up. My brother, the joker, was never angry. Not even when we were in a gun match with the Bratva or Irish.

"Good, I don't want my brother's leftovers."

"You're not marrying Gia," he growled and then caught himself. "She'd make a shitty wife."

"Why'd you guys fall out, Alessandro?" I said softly, my patience wearing thin.

"It doesn't matter." He shook his head, and his eyes widened as he stared at his phone. "I just got a message from Vee. The plan is in action."

"Okay, for Melba's, right?"

"Yup, Melba's pizzeria is hiring two new staff." He grinned. "You took care of your part."

"Of course." I laughed. "His cashflow is zero. We'll have a new employee soon."

"It's too easy. Like drawing a spider to a web."

"Or a lamb to slaughter." I chuckled lightly, then, a sinister sound to even my ears. "By the way, we're not done talking about Gia. I'm not going to push it now, but I want some answers, Alessandro. We don't keep secrets from each other. That's our one rule.

We have to be honest with each other. You hear me?"

"Yes." He nodded, but I knew today was not going to be the day. "Now let's head to Carmine's. I got some singles with a Brazilian girl's name on them."

CHAPTER 18

Callie

"He's more myself than I am. Whatever our souls are made of. His and mine are the same." — Emily Bronte

"**D**ad, it's okay. I can get another job that pays better," I placated my dad, who was staring at me with dismayed puppy dog eyes. "You weren't to know."

"I've had permission to rent out that place for years." He sounded dejected. "I have no idea why they all of a sudden changed the zoning."

"Can you ask someone at the mayor's office?" I asked him hopefully. I'd always known my dad wasn't good with money, but I'd never expected his income source to disappear. "Can we file a complaint?"

"I don't know." He shook his head. "This is all my fault."

"No, Dad." I pat his shoulder to comfort him. "It's not your fault."

"It is." He stared at my face. "You look so much like your beautiful mother." His voice caught. "I was not good enough for her."

"Dad..."

"I took her for granted. I am paying the price for my sins."

"Dad, it's not your fault she got cancer."

"That was not my fault, no." He looked down at his feet. "But I am ashamed of my actions."

"You need to live your life, Dad. Mom would want you to."

"My life is dedicated to you, my darling Callie. Everything I do is for you."

"I know." I didn't know what to say. I didn't know how to tell him that I didn't want to be his reason for living anymore. I needed him to let go. I was strong. I was independent. I could take care of myself. I wanted to be able to fly. I wanted to be able to figure out my path without worrying about him. The irony of the situation was that while my dad had given up his life to take care of me, I felt like I was the one that was taking care of him. "I have to go now, Dad. I have homework. Thanks for lunch."

"Get home safely." He kissed me on the cheek.

"We will figure out how to get you the money you need."

"I know." I gave him a quick hug. What I knew was that I needed to figure it out myself or I'd have to take out even more loans, and I really didn't want to have to do that.

I knew Valentina had been in the room because when I entered I saw a slew of clothes on the ground and a ripped-up piece of paper on the edge of my bed. I hurried over and picked it up. There were a few sentences scrawled in black pen and a kiss made with lipstick. I read the words quickly to see if they offered some clue as to where Valentina had been.

"Hey, Cassie, I'm spending time with Maksim. We're desperately in love. Hope you had fun at the party. You're a doll. Still have your Chanel bag as it's so cute. Valentina."

I pursed my lips at the last line. "I want my bag back, bitch." I was pissed and surprised at the venom in my tone. I'd been half worried that the mafia had kidnapped her for sending me as her, but she was just with her boyfriend. I wanted to scream and shout at her. "Hope you had fun at the party." I read her words out loud in disgust. "Yeah, it was a ball, Valentina. I danced all night and nearly had my head blown off by the mafia boss himself. Thanks for telling me where I was going." I let out a huge grunt and threw her tattered piece of paper to the ground. I then looked at her clothes all over the floor, and frustration seethed at the mess. I reached down and picked them up and threw them onto her mattress. "And don't leave your shit everywhere." I was done with Valentina. She was rude, mean, not a good roommate, and now I had to admit she wasn't even a friend. She was a user, and I wanted nothing more to do with her.

My eyes spied a newspaper on her bedside table. There was another lipstick mark on the paper, and I glanced down. She'd circled a want ad for a job.

"Melba's Pizza is seeking two waitresses and a bartender," the ad read. I was surprised Valentina was looking for a job, but maybe Maksim worked there and she wanted to spend more time with him. Or maybe her parents had found out about the relationship and cut her off. That would serve her right. I felt a little bit guilty for the thought.

I was about to move back to my side of the room, when my mind suddenly recalled the last part of the ad. I turned back around and picked the paper up. "Earn up to six figures." That was a lot of money. And I needed money now that my dad couldn't help me in any way. I had one more semester of tuition to find. And I had to pay for my housing, books, food, and clothes. And I really didn't want to spend my last semester of college living back at home with my dad.

I stared at the ad for a few seconds. Maybe I'd apply to be a waitress or something. I grabbed my phone and called the number quickly before I could overanalyze all the reasons why it would be a bad idea.

"It's a good day at Melba's Pizza," a cheery man with a deep Italian accent answered the phone.

"Hello, I saw the job advertisement…the one that said six figures."

"Job advertisement?" he responded, sounding confused.

"There was an ad in the paper for two waitresses and a bartender."

"Oh, I think we already hired a new bartender here, but if you're looking, I'd try Lupo's. I heard Boss is hiring there."

"Oh, I was actually hoping for the waitress position…" I drifted off. I knew nothing about being a bartender.

"Bartender makes more money," the voice said. "If you wanna be a waitress, come on down. I think the pay starts at fifteen dollars an hour. We split the tips between the waitstaff, bussers, back-of-house, and the boss."

"The boss gets your tips?" I heard the shock in my voice. "Isn't that illegal?"

"Who you working for? The feds?" His attitude

changed, and I realized he'd hung up the phone on me.

"That was weird," I mumbled as I stared at the ad. "Don't want to work for you anyway, Melba." I glared at the newspaper. Maybe the weird man had saved me from working a shitty job and I didn't even know it. I sat down on the edge of my bed and sighed. I needed to find a job. Then I recalled he'd mentioned another restaurant that was hiring. Lupo's. The name sounded familiar, and I wondered if it was the bar I'd walked past the previous week.

I searched in my phone for the number and then called.

"Thank you for calling Lupo's. This is Birgette. Would you like to make a reservation?"

"Hi, I was calling because I heard you might be hiring?"

"Oh wow, they got that ad in the paper fast." She sounded surprised. "The boss only came through yesterday."

"Oh okay, so there are still open positions?"

"Yes." She lowered her voice. "Though I'm not sure I would..." She stopped. "The phone is for you, Lucio." I heard some whispering in the background, and then a man took the phone.

"This is Lucio."

"Uhm, hello, Lucio. My name is Callie Rowney, I'm a senior at NYU, and I was hoping to apply for a job."

"You got experience?"

"Yes." I didn't ask him what sort of experience. It was his job to be clearer in what he was looking for.

"You got one of those resume thingies?"

"Yes," I said. "I have a resume I can email you or I can bring it in for an interview."

"Good, good. When can you start?"

I was surprised by his question. Wasn't he going to set up the interview first?

"Whenever you need me to," I said. "My schedule is pretty open."

"Great. Come in tonight."

"Tonight?" I could hear the shock in my voice. I didn't think I'd be starting that early.

"We'll pay you twenty-five dollars an hour."

"What time should I be there?" I asked him quickly. I'd sell a kidney for twenty-five dollars an hour right about now.

"Five p.m." He paused. "Make it four. You wanna be a bartender, cook, or waitress?"

"I'd say I have the most experience as a waitress." Technically, this was true. I'd brought dishes to the dining room table many times at home and at friends' houses.

"You know how to make drinks? We lost our bartender unexpectedly."

"I know a thing or two." I knew how to pour whiskey and vodka and how to add seltzer, Coke, or Sprite, but he didn't need to know all the details. I would download a drink app before I got to the job. That would tell me everything I needed to know.

"Good." He coughed. "We might need some help in the kitchen as well."

"For twenty-five dollars an hour?" All of a sudden, I wondered if working at Lupo's was going to be a bad idea.

"Fine, fifty dollars an hour, but only because you have so much experience."

My face tinged red, then. Had I blatantly lied to this man? And how was he a hiring manager if he did no due diligence? I didn't know how to respond. I was about to come clean when he said, "You got me, seventy-five dollars an hour." He sighed. "Be here at four… Birgette, put that back on." I heard giggling in the background and my eyebrows raised. What had Birgette taken off? Lupo's sounded like a hot mess, but for seventy-five dollars an hour, I could deal with it. I just needed to save enough money to be financially settled. I was a fast learner and was confident of my abilities. I mean, what could really go wrong? If it was absolutely awful, I would just leave.

"Looks like you have a job, Callie." I squealed as I jumped up and down. Maybe I'd find that I loved working there so much that I'd want to open my own bar one day. Unlikely, but it was a way for me to test future career paths. Though I knew I had to start looking into grad school apps. They were due in the next couple of months, and if I wanted to go right after graduation, I needed to apply now. Could I see myself as a therapist? Did I have the right sort of temperament? I thought back to my meeting with Antonio Marchesi and how I'd reacted to him. What if he'd been my patient? Would I have been so snappy and rude?

"But he wasn't your patient, and he was an obnoxious brute," I reminded myself as I laid back on my bed. I had an hour to rest before I'd have to get ready for my new job. Antonio's brooding brown eyes popped into my mind. He'd been so handsome, even though he'd been a jerk. I wondered what I would have done if he had kissed me. Slapped him, most probably, but I bet he would have liked it. A warm feeling of delight whirled in my stomach at the thought. There was a hint of darkness in Antonio, and while I didn't particularly want a dark man, it did turn me on a little bit.

CHAPTER 19

Antonio

"Murder's out of tune,
And sweet revenge grows harsh." — William Shakespeare.

I laid the roses down on my mother's grave and did a quick sign of the cross. Emilia Marchesi, beloved mother and wife. Died at the young age of thirty. She'd been too young. Everything in her life had happened too fast. She'd married my father at nineteen. Had me at twenty-two. And then died when I was eight. She'd been a wonderful mother. Full of laughter. I could remember her taking me to the park. And ice cream. I could remember her reading bedtime stories to me and Alessandro. She'd make up fairytales with us as the heroes. Alessandro had been younger than I was when she died, but he still remembered the stories. Still tried making them up. I hated it when he did that.

"Papa's looking for you." Alessandro stepped up behind me and lightly touched my shoulder before he laid down his own bouquet of flowers. "Love you, Mama."

We stood there in silence for a few seconds, paying our respects to our mother. I could feel the anger seething in me as I stared at her gravestone. I hated that she was dead. I hated that she'd never gotten to see me grow. Everything I did in life was to avenge her death. I would not let her ending be in vain.

"Papa wants to know if you have a first choice," Alessandro continued, his voice weary, as he stood there all in black.

"What did you say?" I turned to him.

"I couldn't say the truth, obviously."

"Obviously."

"I said you were thinking of Serena."

"He must have loved that."

"Tommasso was there." He smirked at me. "I think he loved it even more."

"She's not even a thought in my head."

"Not even to suck your cock?"

"I can have any girl I want sucking my cock." I smirked. "I don't need her."

"Maybe not the little lamb," he taunted me. "I

don't see her dropping to her knees begging to suck you."

"I don't even know who you're talking about." I folded my arms together, my mind immediately going to Callie in her red dress with her angry brown eyes.

"Uh huh." He laughed and grabbed his phone. "Wanna check out Melba's tonight?"

"Why? Any updates?"

"Vee says the mouse ate the cheese." He grinned. "We can take Jimmy. See if we have any new hires."

"Jimmy's a brute." I thought about it for a moment. "Fine, we can take him."

"I'll call him. He can meet us here?"

"Not at Mama's grave," I said sharply, and Alessandro gave me an admonishing look.

"Of course not."

"Fine. Tell him to meet us at the house in thirty."

"I'll text him now." He nodded. "You want to lead the prayer or should I?"

"I will." I waited for him to send the text and then watched as he slid the phone into his back pocket. His jeans were too fucking tight. They were made for a frigging lady with a tight ass, not his stocky-ass thighs, but I kept my mouth shut. Alessandro considered himself trendy, and I knew I wasn't. If he wanted to wear girl jeans, I'd fucking let him. It hadn't affected his ability to shoot a gun as yet.

"I'm ready." He nodded at me, and we both fell to

our knees next to the grave. The sky was a dark, ominous gray, and the wind was picking up speed as it sailed through the sky and knocked tree branches and leaves to the ground.

"In the name of the father, the son, and the holy spirit, so help us God," I started as I made the sign of the cross. I looked over at Alessandro and saw his eyes were closed, and I continued. "Forgive us, Father, for we have sinned."

"But not as much as we're about to…" he added, and I snorted. His eyes flew open and stared into mine and I shook my head.

"We're going to hell." I stared at him, my own reflection staring back at me from his eyes.

"And we're going to take *him* with us," he continued with a bitter smile and then turned toward the gravestone. "For you, Mama, we're doing it all for you."

CHAPTER 20

Callie

"Love has nothing to do with what you are expecting to get, only with what you are expecting to give—which is everything." — Katharine Hepburn

L upo's. The sign outside the restaurant bar looked brand new. It was a weird sign; the background was a cream white, and the logo was of a dark gray wolf with some sort of skull beneath it. The wolves fangs were bared and biting into the skull, and blood was dripping down to make the name of the store.

"Doesn't even make sense," I mumbled as I walked into the store. A skull didn't have flesh and blood, so a wolf's fangs wouldn't draw blood; they'd draw nothing but maybe some splintered bone shards. I pressed my sweaty palms against my slightly too short black skirt and took a deep breath. "Here goes nothing."

"Welcome to Lupo's. Do you have a reservation?" A cute blond girl smiled at me, and I shook my head.

"Today's my first day…" I hoped it was going to go well.

"Oh, yeah, we spoke on the phone." She giggled. "I'm Birgette."

"Nice to meet you, Birgitte."

"I should have realized you weren't here to eat or drink." She smiled widely at me. "We're not even open yet."

"Oh, okay." I smiled back at her but wondered how she'd forgotten they weren't open yet. There didn't even seem to be anyone else working right now.

"Lucio," she called behind me, contradicting my thought.

"What?" a gruff voice shouted back.

"The new girls here. The restaurant guru gal." She beamed at me as my heart thudded uncomfortably. What the hell was she talking about? Guru? Was she high? The only thing I was a guru of was reality TV dating shows, which I watched out of pleasure and jealousy every chance I could get. Was Shayne a villain? Was Bartise a jerk? Those were questions I could answer. But I barely knew how to set a table. No one in the world would call me a restaurant guru.

"Fine, I'm coming," the voice shouted back, and a few seconds later, a shortish man with jet-black hair and bright blue eyes walked to the front of the restaurant. "Hey, you're the new hire I spoke to?" He looked me up and down.

"Gordon Ramsay, in person," I joked, playing off the restaurant guru comment. However, he didn't seem to get it. Neither did Birgette.

"I didn't know women could be called Gordon," she said, looking confused, and I stifled a giggle.

"I'm Callie. I'm a senior at NYU. Gordon Ramsay is a British chef that also runs restaurants. He's a guru...so I..." I shrugged as they just stared at me blankly. "Cool space you have here."

"Thanks." Lucio nodded. "I'm the manager."

"Practically the owner." Birgette batted her eyelashes at him, and I tried not to look shocked. So there was something going on between them. Birgette was beautiful in a ditzy way, and Lucio looked like a henchman for the mob. In fact, he slightly reminded me of some of the guys I'd seen escorting women into the party. I knew I was over-thinking it because that night had been so over-whelming. I had to stop typecasting people. Every short, stocky, Italian-American-looking man with tattoos, a rough accent, and twitching eyes wasn't in the mafia.

"That's cool," I said quickly. "So do I need to fill out any paperwork or what?"

"Yeah, I guess tax stuff." Lucio frowned. "This is a legit business, you know."

"Uhm, yeah." I nodded quickly. Had he sensed that I'd mentally compared him to a mafia soldier? I blushed slightly at the thought. "I brought my birth certificate and my passport." I held up my handbag. "Oh, and my social security card. Gotta pay Uncle Sam his share, am I right?"

"What, you heard?" Lucio asked suspiciously.

"Huh?" I could feel my Spidey senses kicking in, and something wasn't quite right here. Lucio and Birgette seemed to be Tweedledee and Tweedledum and the most prominent word between the two seemed to be dum with a b. I knew I was being mean, but I couldn't stop myself.

"Nothing." He pulled his shoulders up and rotated them for a few seconds before practicing some boxing jibes. "We'll do the paperwork later. You wanna start in the kitchen?"

"Start what in the kitchen?" I asked him, confused. Was I somehow in the twilight zone? I pinched my right arm and it hurt, so I knew I wasn't dreaming.

"Starters…creating a new appetizer menu. Boss didn't seem happy with tuna tartare and calamari."

"I thought you were the boss."

"I mean the owner." Lucio sounded irritated as if I should have known what he was talking about. I didn't want to say that just two minutes ago, Birgette was going on like he practically owned the place. What sort of manager was he? I was starting to wonder if he was a nepo baby and his daddy had gotten him the job, because there was no way any sane person would have hired him to be manager. Anyone with half a brain could see this guy was an idiot. I mean, he'd hired me without doing an interview, looking at my resume, or contacting any of my references.

"You don't wanna mess with the boss." Birgette wrinkled her nose. "He's scary."

"Uhm okay." I cleared my throat. "Look, I'm not actually sure this is going to work out." I looked back toward the entrance and was about to leave when Lucio stepped in front of me.

"A hundred dollars an hour. We need your expertise." He grunted, and I just stared at him. I had no expertise, but a hundred dollars an hour was a lot of money. "Under the table."

"Oh…is that legal?" I asked stupidly, and he just blinked at me. What did I really have to lose? True, maybe I wasn't an expert, but compared to these two, I would be a major step up. "Who else is working tonight?" I asked.

"Just us." Lucio shrugged. "Fired everyone yesterday."

"Besides me." Birgette smiled, and Lucio nodded, though he looked a little nervous.

"I'm hiring all new people." He stared at me. "You're first in command."

"So tonight it's just us?" I raised an eyebrow at him.

"Yeah, so you good to be in the kitchen for now?"

"What exactly am I supposed to cook?"

"I don't know." He shrugged. "Meatballs, bruschetta, panzanella?"

"Uhm, I can try some meatballs and maybe bruschetta." I nodded. "You have the ingredients?"

"What we don't have, I'll go and buy." He shrugged, and I just stared at him. I had a bad feeling that this wasn't going to go well, but I wasn't in a financial position to care.

"Okay, show me to the kitchen," I said and took a couple of deep breaths as I followed him through the restaurant. The place was actually quite decent looking. There were a lot of plants and natural wood colors. The tables were all two-tops with comfortable-looking purple velvet chairs. Small candles in candlestick holders that looked like hands and fake flowers sat on every table, ruining the otherwise attractive decor of the place. It was a bit of a mismatch, and the giant Italian flag that hung in the center of the room wasn't doing anything for the decor.

"Thank God," I whispered as we entered the kitchen. It was clean and seemed to be well stocked.

If I'd seen a bunch of grease or rat droppings, I would have been out of there.

"That's the fridge." Lucio pointed to a large walk-in fridge at the side of the room. "Check it out and let me know what you need."

"Uhm, okay." I nodded as I pressed my lips together. Thank God I had a phone and internet. I'd have to google some recipes.

"You want a drink?" he asked as he headed back out of the kitchen.

"No, I'm okay, thanks."

"Well, if you change your mind, feel free to help yourself at the bar." He pointed to the front. "We open in about an hour and a half. Once we open, I'll have you move between the front and the back."

"Hmmm?" I stared at him for a few moments. "For what?"

"So you can alternate between making the food and drinks." He stared at me like I was slow. "Birgette is the hostess, and I'm the manager, so you'll have to do the rest."

"Yeah, okay..." Was he crazy? What would they have done if I hadn't called and taken the job? I didn't bother saying anything, though, because I didn't want to annoy him. I had a feeling it wasn't going to be that busy, anyway. The location was good, but Lupo's had a lot of competition with much better-looking places. And they were definitely at the bottom of the rung.

"Two more meatballs on toast," Lucio opened the door and shouted. "And a Caesar salad." He was gone before I could respond. I'd been wrong about the lack of business. We weren't packed, but we did have customers. And they were ordering food in droves. I stared down at the apron I'd found. It was covered in flour and red marinara sauce. I stared at the silver bowl in front of me and shook my head. Time to make more meatballs.

I threw two packages of ground beef and ground pork into the bowl. And then looked back on my phone.

"Salt, pepper, oregano, pepper flakes, garlic, onion, thyme, parmesan, and egg." I repeated the words out loud to see if I could burn them into my brain. My fingers dug into the meat and combined all the ingredients together.

The smoke alarm started beeping, and I cursed under my breath. The french bread that I'd put into the oven to toast was burning. "Fuck it, fuck it."

I grabbed a tea towel and wiped my hands quickly and opened the oven and pulled out the blacked tops of bread. I'd scrape the charcoal parts off and pray that no one hated the taste.

I grabbed the giant bottle of extra virgin olive oil and poured it into the frying pan before stirring the pot of marinara sauce that was bubbling on the stovetop, thanks to Bertinelli's. What a sham I was.

My phone started ringing then. It was Josh. I had no idea why he was calling me, but I didn't have time to find out. I grabbed a spoon and divided up the meat and rolled them into balls. They looked and smelled good, so that was something. I was about to drop the meatballs into the pan when the phone started ringing again. I pressed accept and then speakerphone.

"Hey, Josh, what's going on?" I asked as I dropped four meatballs into the searing-hot pan. The meat sizzled as it cooked, and I pushed the meatballs to the side so that I could add a few more to the pan.

"Where are you, Callie?" he asked in a flirtatious voice, and I frowned in surprise.

"At work, why?"

"I just was wondering if you wanted to grab a pizza or something?"

"Uhm, I'm at work, so no."

"Oh, okay, when do you get off?"

"Why?"

"I don't know. Figured we could go on a date or something." His voice trailed off. "I mean, we haven't hung out in a while."

"Hey, Josh, can I call you back?" The sauce was bubbling over the top of the pot now. I needed to turn the heat down.

"Oh, okay." He sounded disappointed. "You'll call

me back?"

"Yeah, sure." I hung up, even though I had no real clue as to why he was calling me. Was he hoping for a repeat of "Falling Asleep Between My Legs Gate?" Because if that was the case, he'd have a long time to wait.

"Those meatballs ready?" Lucio sounded harassed as he walked back into the kitchen and stalked over to me.

"Nearly." I didn't even look at him. "I can only cook so fast." I flipped the meatballs over and grabbed a knife to scrape the burned bits off before placing them on plates.

"What's that?" He sniffed and looked down at the slightly less burned toast tops.

"The bread for the meatball toast."

"Why does it look like that?"

"Because I'm not Wolfgang frigging Puck." I grabbed some paper towels and placed them on the counter and then took out the meatballs. They were soaked in oil and didn't look very appetizing, but I figured the marinara sauce would cover how ugly they looked. What a mess.

"I'll finish this," he said. "Can you go to the bar? Some customers want to order cocktails."

"You can't serve them?"

"I only know beer."

"Okay." I was about to take my apron off but then said fuck it. I walked out to the front of the bar and saw a crowd of about ten people all waiting for drinks. "Fuck my life." I groaned as I avoided eye contact and walked behind the bar top. I caught sight of my reflection in the mirrored glass wall, and I looked like a hot mess. My hair was frizzy, and there was flour all over my face as well. My makeup had melted off, and my attire was a hot mess. I could see Birgette standing at the stand near the front entrance looking cool and unbothered, and it struck me that this whole setup was terribly unfair. I was being treated like Cinderella. Granted, I was making a hundred dollars an hour, but this was just too much.

"Hi, welcome to Lupo's," I said in a half-hearted tone to the two preppy guys standing at the front of the bar. "What can I get you to drink?"

"Two Moscow Mules, bitch," the guy in the pinstriped suit responded with a sneer. "How many times do we have to place the same order?"

My jaw dropped at his comment. I was pissed off. And not just because he'd called me a bitch. But I had no idea what a Moscow Mule was, and I'd left my phone in the kitchen.

"Coming right up, jackass." I smiled sweetly at him, and it was his turn to be shocked. I didn't care. What was Lucio going to do? Fire me? Unlikely. I grabbed a glass and a bottle of liquor. I'd make my own creation and just say this was the Lupo's special Mule, for jackasses like him, if he complained.

CHAPTER 21

Antonio

"The best sort of revenge is not to be like him who did the injury." — Marcus Antoninus

"What did you say to me?" The Wall Street prick sounded affronted, and I wanted to slap him. Alessandro and I were staring at each other in shock. The little lamb was standing behind the bar, serving drinks in our bar. This was unexpected. I'd expected to see her at Melba's and been disappointed when she hadn't been there. I'd thought the plan had failed. But here she was. I didn't know how or why, but it seemed like fate was playing right into my hands.

"Here you go," she snapped as she slammed a glass down on the counter in front of her. "A

Moscow Mule for…" She paused as the man glared at her.

"This isn't vodka," the man bellowed. "It tastes like gin."

"It's the house special," she responded quickly, and I chuckled inwardly. This wasn't the sort of service I wanted in my bar, but I had to appreciate that she knew how to handle herself. The little lamb was spunky and not just with me. I was surprised. This was a side of her personality I hadn't expected to see. She hadn't noticed me or Alessandro yet. I wondered how she would react when she saw me. Would she recognize me? I smirked at the thought. There was no way she could have forgotten me. And I knew I'd left an impression on her when I'd packed her into the limo and sent her on her way.

She'd been expecting something else to happen. She'd been expecting to be devoured. Her eyes had been begging me to kiss her. Her breathing had been labored. She'd wanted to be touched and to touch. I'd wanted to give her what she wanted, but I'd had to be patient. And my patience had paid off, because here she was.

"You want me to say something, boss?" Jimmy's voice was eager. He loved a punch-up, and the Wall Street douche was looking like he needed a good punch.

"No." I shook my head and looked around. "Where the hell is Lucio?"

"Who knows?" Alessandro looked back toward Birgette. "At least we know they're not fucking on company time."

"We don't know that." I pursed my lips. Lucio was doing a shit job, and I knew I was going to have to fire him, but I was intrigued to hear how little miss Callie had gotten this job. "Let's sit over there." I nodded to Jimmy and Alessandro. "You two take a seat. I got this."

"You sure, boss?" Jimmy was disappointed.

"I got it." I watched as Lucio head out of the kitchen with two plates. I could feel anger setting in as I stared at them. Red sauce was splattered all over the plate. There were two pieces of burned bread on one corner next to two soggy-looking meatballs and a splatch of what looked like store-bought sauce. Lucio sauntered past me, not even noticing me there as he placed the dishes on a table behind me. Two women sat there looking disappointed at the dishes they'd been served, but Lucio didn't seem to notice.

"Hey, Cassie," he said as he headed toward the bar. "Pull me a beer."

"I'm making these drinks," she snapped, her eyes shooting darts at him.

"Hmph." He looked at the crowd in front of me, and then suddenly he spotted me. "Oh hey, boss, I didn't know you were coming in tonight." He hurried over to me, looking sheepish.

"I can tell."

"I hired a new girl. A guru she is. They call her Wolfgang fucking Puck or something," he mumbled as he nodded back to a frazzled Callie. "She's going to put us on the map."

"She's a guru?"

"Yeah." He nodded enthusiastically. "She's got a resume, knows how to cook, make drinks, everything." He grinned. "She's a bit expensive, but I said we pay for the best, right, boss?"

"Hmm." I stared at him, wondering exactly what was going on. Had Callie said she had all this experience? I already knew she could lie well under pressure. Well, not well, but it would be easy to fool Lucio. Or had Lucio fucked up again and just hired another pretty face?

"You want me to introduce you?" He was about to head back to the bar when I grabbed him by the shoulder.

"Nah. I got it." I stepped forward, ready to take charge. The Wall Street prick was getting loud again, and I knew I had to take care of the situation before everyone started feel uncomfortable. "Hey, excuse me, what seems to be the problem?" I said loudly, asserting my dominance as I stood next to the bar. "I'm the owner."

I heard a loud gasp as Callie finally saw me. I turned to her unsmiling, taking in her appearance, her trembling lips, her nervous eyes.

"Why hello, little lamb. We meet again."

"You." She pointed at me. "What...what are you doing here?"

"I'm your new boss," I said in a cold voice. "And this time, I'm not going to let you leave so easily." I walked toward the back of the bar, and my throat constricted as I took in her long, shapely legs in their black stockings. She was wearing a short skirt and short heels, and even though the dirty apron covered her top half, she looked stunning. She was totally unlike the put-together women I was used to, but that drew me into her more. I moved closer to her until I was too close for polite company. She looked up at me with wide eyes, a shyness suddenly crossing over her face.

"You're in my space." She glared at me, and I laughed.

"I'm about to be in a lot more than that." I winked at her, and she blushed. The wolf was on the way to getting his little lamb, and I was more than ready for what was going to happen next.

CHAPTER 22

Callie

"A loving heart is the truest wisdom." — Charles Dickens

O h my God. My brain was racing as I stared at Antonio "The Wolf" Marchesi. Was this real? He owned Lupo's. I couldn't believe it. Turned out my stereotyping of Lucio hadn't been so wrong after all. He was affiliated with the mob. Shit, now I was also affiliated. I was working for a mafia boss. I mean, I hadn't known it, and there was no way I would have taken the job. But I had to admit that he looked good. Even more handsome than I'd remembered, but maybe it was because we were in better light here under the bar.

His brown eyes were laughing at me as he stood there, his face haughty and obnoxious as he smirked at me. He was taller than I remembered. And his body appeared more muscular. His biceps were practically bulging in the black shirt he was wearing. And he smelled good. Like aged barrels of whiskey and cedar. I tried not to sniff him like a weirdo, but his smell was oddly intoxicating.

"Why are you here?" I finally found my words again after his very sexual innuendo.

"Looks like you didn't win the brains lottery, huh, Wolfgang?" He smirked, and I resisted the urge to stick my tongue out at his words. "Like I just said, I'm the boss, and I own this place."

"Are you following me?"

"I think the right question should be are you stalking me?" He tapped his finger against the bartop. "As in you stalking and following me...this is my bar, after all."

"No, I'm not stalking you. Why would I want to stalk you?" I rolled my eyes at him.

"I don't know. You saw my hot body and handsome face and figured you had to have me." He shrugged nonchalantly, but I could see his lips twitching. He was really full of himself, wasn't he?

"Uhm, I've yet to see a hot boy or handsome face anywhere near you," I lied. "All I see is an ego and big nose."

"Big nose?" He touched his nose and laughed. "Nice comeback, little lamb."

"Oh look, the big bad wolf is here to intimidate me." I glared at him.

"Are you going to get my fucking drink order ready?" the preppy asshole at the bar shouted, and I watched as Antonio walked toward him and grabbed him around the collar.

"I think the only thing that's going to happen right now is that you're going to leave," he said in a calm tone. "Before things get interesting." He took a step back and brought the guy halfway across the bartop. My eyes widened at the action. He was strong. Preppy guy's mouth was closed now. As were his friends's. Antonio's grip tightened, and he continued. "Apologize to the lady... It's her first day."

"Sorry," the guy spluttered out, coughing. Antonio let go of his grip, and the guy went falling back. "Let's go." He turned to his friends, and they exited.

"You didn't have to act like a thug. I was handling it."

"You were handling it?" He raised an eyebrow. "With a gin Moscow Mule?"

"It was my own variation."

"Russians are known for vodka. Moscow is in Russia." He stared at me.

"I know that." I rolled my eyes. "Like I said, it was my own version of a Moscow Mule."

"Called what? The 'I don't know how to make drinks' version?"

"I do know," I lied.

"Fine. Make me a Singapore Sling then."

"Coming right up," I said, staring at him defiantly. "Actually, you know what? I quit. I'm not working for you."

"Oh yeah?" He grabbed a hold of my arm. "So you're a quitter?"

"I don't work for mobsters."

He burst out laughing, then. "Is that all you think of me?" He tilted his head to the side and studied my face. "You crash my party for free drinks and food, but now I'm not good enough to work for?"

"I didn't even know it was your party." She ran her fingers through her hair and frowned. "I told you. I was helping out a friend."

"Oh yeah, the Westside Story drama."

"I said Romeo and Juliet, but yeah same sort of story." She wrinkled her nose. "Valentina wasn't able to attend or rather she didn't want to, and now I know why."

"Sure you do." He licked his lips, and I saw him staring at my mouth. Fuck it, but he had kissable lips. I wondered if they would taste as sweet as they looked. *Focus, Callie, you are not going to daydream about kissing a mob boss.*

"Whatever, I'm not talking to you anymore, Antonio." I took off my apron and threw it at him. Oops! I looked down and noticed that some of the red marinara sauce had stained his top. "I'm out."

"I don't think so." He shook his head. "Or do you not honor your commitments?"

"What commitments?" I made a face. I knew this man wasn't going to guilt me into staying when he had hired a manager that was literally an idiot. "I literally started this job today, and I think you have bigger issues than me."

"Oh yeah? Like what?"

"Like your manager." I pursed my lips together and looked toward the front of the restaurant, where Lucio and Birgette were flirting with each other. They looked like they were ready to go into the stockroom and bang any minute. "Lucio…" I paused. "Whatever his last name is."

"What are you talking about?" Antonio looked confused and moody, and I just couldn't believe that he was standing here in front of me. It had been less than a week since I'd seen him, and yet here he was showing up in my life again.

"It doesn't matter," I said, shaking my head. "Please pay me what you owe me, so I can go home."

"You'll go home when we close."

"I think not." He really was used to having too much power if he thought I was just going to obey his every word.

"I think yes. We'll serve our customers, and then I will give you a ride home."

"Ha!" I burst out laughing, then. "You think I'm going to let you take me home?"

"Why wouldn't you?" He took a step closer to me. "Are you worried I'll kidnap you and have my wicked way with you?"

"You wouldn't dare." I jutted my chin up and narrowed my eyes.

"I wouldn't?" His lips were thin, and his eyes darkened. "You really don't know who you're talking to, do you?"

"So you're saying you would take me against my will?"

"Never," he spat out distastefully. "But I would make it so that was all your will wanted."

"What are you talking about?" I rolled my eyes at him.

"I bet that after just one date with me, you will want me to have my wicked way with you."

"You're full of yourself." I laughed in his face. "We could go on ten dates, and I still would have no interest. I'm not interested in mob bosses. Or arrogant assholes. Or a man whose ego is bigger than his..." I looked down to his pants. "You know what."

"You know what?" He threw his head back and laughed. "You are a little lamb, aren't you? Are you scared to say dick?"

"No." I blushed.

"Then say it." His eyes were alive with mischief. "Say that you think my ego is bigger than my thick, fat, juicy, eight-inch cock." He leaned forward and whispered in my ear. "And if you don't believe me, try to stuff it in your mouth."

I gasped at his words, even as my body shivered at the breath he'd blown into my ear. My entire body was trembling now, and my knees felt weak. I stared at his cocky face, and something akin to anger coursed through me. Before I knew what I was doing, my hand was moving and slapping him across the face.

"Don't you ever talk to me like that again," I hissed at him. "I am a lady, and I will not have you disrespecting me like that." Respect flashed in his eyes for a few seconds before his expression changed.

"If you do that again, you won't like what happens next."

"What's that supposed to mean?" I rolled my eyes at him. Was he threatening me? He nodded behind me, and I turned to look over my shoulder. A skinny dude with big blue eyes and a weirdly attractive face was standing there, a gun in his hand pointed at me. My heart almost stopped. "So now your men are going to kill me because I called you out for being a rude ass?"

"What did I say that was so rude?" He shrugged and then rose his voice as he shook his head. "It's fine, Jimmy."

"You sure, boss?" Jimmy sounded riled up as he walked over to us. He looked me up and down and then looked at Antonio. "You want me to teach her a lesson?"

"You won't touch her," Antonio hissed, a sudden flash of violence in his tone that made me shiver. "Sit down."

"Yes, boss." I heard him moving away from me.

"And you wonder why I don't want to work here anymore." I shook my head. "This is why."

"Why?" He looked annoyed. "Because I have a security guard?"

"He's not exactly a security guard, is he?" I shook my head. "You're not exactly the president or Brad Pitt."

"No, but I am Antonio Marchesi." He smirked. "I wield my own power. And I get what I want."

"Well, good for you." I wasn't sure why I was still entertaining this conversation with him. I knew I should leave. In fact, my brain was screaming at me to get out of there. However, I had to admit that I was intrigued by this man. He was everything that I was meant to run from. He was admittedly a mafia boss. Which meant he was a criminal. Which meant he was a bad boy. Which meant he was the sort of man I should want nothing to do with. But there was something about him and our banter that made me want to stay. I'd been so fed up with the boys at university. I'd been wanting to meet a real man. And here he was. Antonio was tall, dark, and handsome. He was the epitome of every single one of those words. I'd been waiting all my life for an adventure. A man that would sweep me off of my feet. Imogen always said you needed a bad boy once in your life to appreciate the good ones. And Antonio was as bad as you could get. The only problem was he was more than just a bad boy. He was dangerous. He was dark. And I honestly didn't know what he was capable of.

"And I want you, Callie Rowney." The words slithered off of his mouth in a venomous way that made a chill run up my spine. Something about what he'd said rang warning bells in my ear, but I wasn't sure what it was.

"That's a pity for you then because I don't want you." I decided to listen to my Spidey senses. "You better focus on the women at your party because I'm just not interested. My father always told me to trust my gut, and well, it's telling me you're bad news."

"Your father sounds like a smart man," he said, nodding, sounding thoughtful. "I'm sure he'd hate to see you with someone like me."

"Most probably." I nodded.

"And you'd hate to disappoint Daddy Dearest, wouldn't you?" He grabbed a bottle of whiskey and poured himself a shot. "You're a good little girl, aren't you?"

"I'm a woman, and I made my own decisions." I pressed my lips together. "I don't make all my decisions based on my dad."

"Then give me one date," he said softly. "If you hate it, I'll never ask again."

"I don't know." I shook my head, wanting to say yes.

"One date and stay working here." His dark eyes bore into mine. "Help me make this place what it could be."

"Why?" I asked him softly, not understanding why he wanted me to stay so badly.

"Because I feel drawn to you," he said softly. "I feel like fate has brought us together. I feel like there has to be a reason we've met twice in a week now." He stepped forward and touched the side of my face. "You have to admit you feel this chemistry between us. You can't deny it. Maybe you'll be the softness that can bring me to the good side." His voice was husky as he touched the small of my back. "Let me take you home. I'll close the bar early tonight."

"I don't know." I shook my head. "I have a room-mate and…"

"I just want to see you get home safely." He smiled. "I just want to start over. We had a weird start. I'm not all bad."

I stared at the sincerity in his eyes, and I could feel my heart skipping. Everything he was saying was music to my romantic ears. Could I be the woman that made him change? Would he leave a life of crime away for me? It was weird that we'd met up twice in just a week.

"But what about your wife hunt?" I said, almost whispering now.

"That's for my father," he said softly, smiling sweetly at me now. "If I meet my true love, I will walk away." His lips pressed against my cheek softly. "I know I can be a brute, but just give me one chance, little lamb. Let me sweep you off of your feet. Let me show you the world. I promise you won't regret it."

"Okay," I said, nodding without thinking it through. "One date." I pressed my fingers to my lips. "And if I don't like what you do or say, it's done."

"But you'll still work for me?" he asked hopefully. "At least we can still be friends?"

"Fine," I said, nodding, touched that my presence in his life meant so much to him. "But you're paying me one hundred dollars an hour, and you can't go back on that."

"Fine," he said with a sheepish grin. "You win, Callie. You strike a hard bargain, but you win this round."

I laughed at his acquiescence and felt a warmth filling me. "I told you that I don't play, Antonio. I might just be a college senior, but my dad has taught me my worth." He nodded and ran his hands through his hair before turning away from me and signaling something to Lucio.

"Go and get yourself cleaned up," he said in a dominant voice. "I'll take care of everything else."

"Okay." I nodded and hurried to the kitchen to grab my stuff. As I got to the door, I turned around to observe his face and body language. He walked over to his brother Alessandro and Jimmy and said something to them. My breath caught as I watched him pulling out his gun and saying something. I wasn't sure if I made a loud noise because suddenly he turned to look toward me, his eyes hooded as he stared at me. He wasn't smiling, and I wondered what he was thinking. Even more, I wondered what I was thinking. Was I playing with fire giving him a shot? What did I really know about this man? He seemed to be able to switch on and off like a light switch, and a part of me wondered if I wasn't completely out of my depth.

CHAPTER 23

Antonio

"*Revenge is a virus which eats into the very vitals of the mind and poisons the entire spiritual being.*" — James Allen

"You need to call Vee," I commanded Alessandro as we stood there.

"What the hell is going on?" he asked me, his eyes searching mine. "And why am I calling Valentina? I thought she was done with her part."

"I need to make sure she doesn't go back to that dorm." I shrugged. "Tell her to continue staying at Maksim's."

"Okay." Alessandro nodded and pulled out his phone. "Anything else?"

"No." I shook my head. "Jimmy, clean out the bar. And tell Lucio this is his last week." I pressed my lips together. "I'll be spending the next couple of weeks here."

"Yes, boss." He looked back toward the kitchen. "You need me to drive you two back?"

"No." I reached my hand out to him. "Give me the keys. You and Alessandro can catch a ride with Lucio."

"But, boss," Jimmy started to protest, and I gave him a look. "Okay, boss." He knew better than to argue with me. "What should I tell your dad about Tommasso and the dinner tomorrow?"

"I'll be there." I didn't have time for this bullshit. "Just text me the details."

"Okay, and there's been some trouble at some of the check-cashing places in the Bronx." He grunted. "I think the Bratva have been sending people in with counterfeit money to pay us back."

"Any proof?"

"Just a hunch," he said. "I told you I've been seeing Dima hanging around the two joints near the subway station with some of his men."

"Fucking Dima, I should have shot him when I had the chance." I grimaced. "How much has come through?"

"Two hundred grand."

"Take care of it. Tell me if it's going to be a bigger problem."

"Yes, boss." He took a step back, and I turned around. Callie was back out of the kitchen and was standing behind me with a nervous expression on her face. She looked good enough to eat. And I was hungry. She was a pretty girl. With more spunk than I'd thought. But she was a typical woman. Wanting to believe that the love of a good woman could change a man like me. That was the problem with women. They let love and the search for true love erase their better instincts. How many times would a woman go against her own gut hoping that a bad man would end up being better than he was?

"You ready?" I reached to grab her hand, but she moved it away from me. So she hadn't gone completely soft, then. A better man than me would have felt bad for lying. But then a better man than me wouldn't be Antonio Marchesi. I wasn't called a wolf for no reason. I was going to eat her up and enjoy it. And when I was done with her, I'd leave nothing but a bunch of bones.

"Are we going?" she said, a slight attitude in her voice, and I knew I couldn't wait for the moment we were intimate. Once I had her naked little body in my arms, I'd put her over my lap and spank that ass until she begged for mercy, and then I'd fuck her so hard that she wouldn't be able to walk for days. I'd show her what she could do with her attitude. She had no idea who she was playing with.

"In a hurry for me to kiss you?" I asked her, with a curl of my lips. I had to admit that I very much wanted to taste her lips.

"Nope." She looked away from me.

"You really are a liar, aren't you?"

"Not at all." She looked back at me. "I just don't really care about kissing you."

"I can't wait for the moment I kiss you and you melt into my arms." I moved closer to her, invading her space. Pressing my body against hers. She shifted slightly but didn't move away.

"Am I a snowman and didn't know it?" she said, raising her eyes to me. And I let out a small laugh. She was quick-witted. I liked that.

"I don't know, are you?" I slid my arm around her waist and pulled her into me. "Shall we check now?"

"I think not." She pursed her lips together. "Let's go now or I'm going to catch a train."

"You're not getting on the subway by yourself at this time of night," I growled at her. "That's not safe."

"It's fine. I take the subway all the time at night by myself."

"Not anymore, you don't." I glared at her. Was her father a fool, letting her travel in the city by herself at night? For an overprotective man, he had surely given her way too much freedom.

"You can't tell me what to do." She made a move toward the door, and I grabbed her arm.

"Fine, I won't." I held in a sigh. "Let's go."

"You can take me home, but don't think anything is going down," she said with a blush. "Because it won't be."

"I'll be a perfect gentleman," I said with a small bow before leaning down to whisper in her ear. I let my tongue circle her earlobe for a few seconds while my hand lightly rubbed her ass. She gasped slightly at my touch, and then I kissed on the back of her neck before moving my lips back up. "I'll only eat you out tonight if you want me to. So just let me know, baby. You can even sit on my face, if that's what you want. You can control the pressure and ensure I shut up at the same time." I could feel her body trembling as I pulled back, and her eyes were wide as she looked back at me. I licked my lips slowly, my gaze never leaving hers. "All you have to do is say the word..." I winked at her. "And my tongue will do your bidding."

CHAPTER 24

Callie

"The one thing we can never get enough of is love. And the one thing we never give enough of is love." — Henry Miller

"Any music you'd like to listen to?" Antonio asked me as we drove down the surprisingly empty streets of the city.

"Not really." I shook my head and stared out of the window. I was still discombobulated by his comments from earlier in the evening. While his innuendos turned me on, I was starting to find them annoying. Was sex all he was interested in? Yes, I wanted physical pleasure, but I also wanted a man that was going to stimulate me mentally and emotionally. As much as I'd hated my experience with Josh, if that was all Antonio had to offer, then I wasn't interested.

"You're annoyed at me?" He sounded surprised, and I let out a low shriek as he pulled over suddenly and slammed on the brakes. "Why are you mad at me now, Callie?"

"Who said I was mad at you?" I shook my head. "You're a rather sensitive man, aren't you? Are you a wolf or a mouse?"

"You've got a smart tongue…" He purred as he unbuckled his seat belt and leaned back to grab something from the backseat. "But you might be a little too quick-witted for your own good."

"Says who?" My heart thudded as I stared at the white rope in his hands. "What's that for?"

"Wouldn't you like to know?" He laughed as he started wrapping it around his hand.

"Are you going to kidnap me?" How could I have been such a dumbass to get into the car with him? I reached for my phone and mentally debated between calling Imogen or my dad. Imogen was too far away to help, but my dad would never let me be alone again if he got a call of distress from me this late at night. His overprotectiveness would kick into two hundred percent. And while I understood why he was that way, I couldn't continue living like a fragile doll. I wasn't my mom. I didn't have cancer. I wasn't going to die. One day, yes, but not now, hopefully.

"If the answer was yes, would I tell you?" He looked at me with a disappointed glance. "Come on now, little lamb, I thought you were smarter than that."

"Well, I thought I was smarter than I am, too. I don't know why I got in a car with you. I can just see the reporters now: 'Why did you get into a car with a known mafia boss?'" I put on a high-pitched TV anchor's voice. "And I'll be like, 'Because I thought he was hot and—'" I gasped as Antonio's lips pressed down on mine, his fingers gripping the sides of my face. I could feel the coarseness of the rope pressing into my cheek, but I didn't hate it. His tongue circled mine, and I sucked on it eagerly. He tasted like whiskey: earthy, sweet, and sour all at the same time. I breathed in his scent as my fingers moved to his hair. My heart was racing so fast I thought it would pop out of my chest, and my skin was on fire. When Antonio finally moved away, I felt like I was gasping for air. His very presence and kiss had sucked all of the oxygen out of me. The feeling was unreal. I felt like I was floating in the air and looking down at my own body. I could hear every sound in the distance: the horns in the distance, the rats running out of the gutters, his beating heat, my own heart ready to stop. I could taste him on my lips still. Antonio was not only handsome, but he had charisma, magnetism, total dominance.

"You got into the car with me for that," he said in

a smug tone, his eyes surveying my still-parted lips with satisfaction. I reached up and touched his lips softly, and he blinked in surprise. "What are you doing?"

"Just checking to see if those things are real." I grinned up at him, and he laughed.

"So you enjoyed it, then?" He cocked his head to the side, his eyes narrowed.

"Yes." I nodded slightly, and I could see the surprise in his eyes. "What?"

"I expected you to say you hated it. That you were going to call the police for me daring to touch you."

"I'm not a liar." I shook my head and then paused. "Well, not most of the time."

"Only to help friends?"

"Valentina's not really a friend," I admitted. "She's just my roommate. I thought we'd be friends, especially after I did her this favor, but I haven't even seen her since that night."

"Weird." He touched the side of my face. "Yet you went to a party and pretended to be her?"

"I'm too nice." I sighed. "When she told me her sob story about her love life, I just wanted to help."

"Aw yes." He nodded. "Vee can be a good actress."

"What?" I frowned. "What do you mean?"

He stared at me for a few seconds. "Teenagers and women in their early twenties are always very overdramatic. I was just talking generally."

"Oh, okay." I couldn't tell if I was being paranoid, but there were several comments he'd made to me recently that struck something in me.

"Let's not talk about your roommate, though." He ran his fingers down my cheek toward my lips. "Let's talk about us."

"What us?" I stared at him in confusion. "You mean about our kiss?"

"I mean I want to talk about our date. Where shall we go?"

"I don't know." I shrugged. "Please not to Central Park. I can't tell you how many dates I've been on in Central Park."

"Oh?" He frowned. "With whom?"

"With guys I was dating, obviously." I giggled. "The last guy I went with was so cheap, he brought a loaf of Wonder Bread and some peanut butter in a Ziploc bag and said to pretend we were in Paris by the Seine." I could barely stop from laughing as I recounted the story, but I noticed that Antonio didn't seem to be laughing. "It was such a bad date," I continued. "Then he tried to kiss me and he had peanut butter stuck to his front tooth and..." My voice trailed off as Antonio's expression grew darker. "What?"

"I don't want to hear about your other men, Callie."

"My other men?" My jaw dropped. "What? I was just telling you about—"

"Do you want to hear about my last date and how she fell to her knees and unzipped me and then—"

"Gross!" I put my hand up and wrinkled my nose at him. "I don't want to hear that." I stared at his laughing eyes and wondered if he was playing games with me. Obviously I knew he had a past. Most probably a very colorful past. I bet he'd done things I'd never even heard of. But I didn't want to hear about them or even think about them. He'd most probably had hundreds of women go down on him, and I'd never even gone down on one man. Not that I was going to tell him that. I wasn't going to have him making fun of me.

"Exactly, you don't want to hear about my sex life. And I don't want to hear about yours."

"A gross peanut butter kiss is not the same as some hoe sucking you off." I glared at him, and he burst out laughing.

"Why's she got be a hoe?" He played with the rope again. "Maybe she just enjoys giving head."

"I don't want to hear about it."

"Let's get you home, little lamb."

"So you're not going to use the rope, then?"

"Not tonight." He grinned and dropped it into his lap. I stared at it, wondering why he had it in his car. But it felt like it wouldn't be smart to ask that question. Did I really want to know the answer? What if he said it was to tie people up with before he dropped them in the river? Or before he beat them to a pulp for betraying him and giving info to the police? I didn't want to know. I didn't want to think about how violent he could be. It suddenly struck me that he may have killed a man. All breath left me, and I suddenly felt cold. Could I really go on a date with someone that may be a murderer?

"You just froze again." He sighed. "What's going through your brain now, little lamb?"

"Nothing." I shook my head. *I don't want to know. I don't want to know. But I kinda do want to know. Just a little bit. A teensy-weensy bit.* "Well, I was just wondering, and you totally don't have to answer this question, but it was on my mind, and I was just thinking…" I took a deep breath. I was scared to ask.

"No, Callie, I'm not a virgin," he said in a monotone voice and then started laughing as he reached over and played with my hair. "Is that what you wanted to know?"

"No." I stuck my tongue out at him. "I think I figured that one out all by myself."

"Smartypants."

"Jerk."

"This is starting to feel like the preamble to hate sex." He winked at me, and I could feel myself blushing. "You'd slap me, and I'd grab your wrists and push you up against the wall. Then you'd hit my chest, while simultaneously taking off my shirt, and I'd pull your arms up above your head. And your nipples would harden as they brushed against my muscular chest, and then I'd lean down and suck on one of them. And you'd shift your stance because your panties would become so wet that you'd think you'd just stepped into the ocean. And then I'd let my hardness..." He cleared his throat. "Also known as my eight-inch wolf push up against your stomach, and then you'd push me back, and my teeth would fall to your neck..." His lips pressed against my neck then, and I wanted to tell him to continue. I wanted to hear about the hot hate sex we'd have. I was a pussy cat for this man. "But then again, I don't think that was your question, right?" He sat back in his seat and started the engine again and pulled out abruptly. "Ask me while I drive you home."

I stared at his hands on the steering wheel, feeling bereft and slightly pissed. I felt like he'd taken me on a mountain hike and then said we had to turn around before we hit the summit. I wanted to see the view! Asshole.

"Have you ever killed someone?" I asked him softly and waited for him to growl or say something rude, but instead he just laughed. "What's so funny?"

"What sort of question is that?" He shook his head and then turned on the radio. Ironically, The Killers blasted into the car, and I started laughing.

"So you're not going to tell me." I was pissed now.

"Do you really want to know?" he asked in a low voice.

"Yes," I mumbled, though I wasn't sure that was the answer I wanted to give.

"I'm a mafia underboss. I will one day be Don. I'm known as the wolf." He paused. "What would your best guess be?"

"You're too sweet to even kill a fly?" I answered him sarcastically.

"You got it." He pulled up on the street, a block from my dorm, and turned off the radio. "I will say that I've never killed someone who didn't deserve it. No innocents have died at my hand." His eyes gazed into mine. "I claim no blood that should not have been shed. I can sleep at night."

"Okay." I nodded. He was talking like he was responsible for honorable killings, but to me a death was a death. "I'm glad you can sleep at night."

"You're not happy with my answer?"

"I mean, I don't really love it, no."

"I haven't taken a mother from her innocent sons." He fingers tapped against the steering wheel. "I haven't caused deep, wrecking isolation and sorrow."

"How do you know that, though?" I made a face. "In your eyes, the people you killed it deserved it, but maybe they had mothers, fathers, children, families that miss them? Maybe they were loved. Who are you to be judge and executioner?"

"I am Antonio Marchesi." His voice held pride and his nostrils flared.

"But you're not God," I said softly, opening the car door. "You don't get to decide who is good and who is bad. You don't get to decide who gets to live."

"I don't take life for fun." He reached out and grabbed my arm. "Wait."

"For what?" I watched as he jumped out of the car and raced over to open my door for me. "You didn't have to do that."

"You're a lady. I am a gentleman." He held his hand out to me. "I will treat you with respect."

"Uh huh."

"So tell me, little lamb, where shall we have our first date?" He held my hand and squeezed it. "And please no stories about Central Park."

"Why don't you take me to France, then?" I said mischievously. "Really show that man up. Take me to the real Seine, buy me an actual French baguette and fromage and real croissants made with butter." I giggled. "Now that would be a first date."

"You want to go to Paris?" he asked me seriously. "You have a passport?"

"I was just joking, Antonio," I said hurriedly. "We're not going to Paris for a date." A first date in Paris sounded very romantic, but I knew that there would be expectations that came with such a date. It was unlikely he'd be booking two rooms and sleeping by himself. And while I felt like he wouldn't be such a bad man to lose my virginity to, I didn't want it to be on the first date.

"Not romantic enough?" He laughed as he pulled me into his arms.

"Too romantic," I admitted. "First date needs to be less pressure, just in case."

"In case of what?" He raised an eyebrow.

"In case it's boring and I want to feign a headache and go home." I tried to ignore the butterflies in my stomach as his hands moved up and down the sides of my body.

"That would never happen," he said confidently.

"Well, just in case." I shrugged. "Lowkey first date."

"You still haven't said where."

"Surprise me." I leaned up on tippytoes and gave him a quick kiss on the lips. "Good night, Antonio. I have to go to bed now." I stepped back and smiled at him. "And no, that's not an invitation."

"I'll pick you up tomorrow morning," he said softly, his eyes veiled as he glanced down at me.

"I have class."

"Skip it," he commanded.

"My dad would love that." I made a face but then nodded. "But fine."

"Good," he said with a small smile. "Be here at seven a.m. and wear a dress."

"A dress?" I raised an eyebrow. "Why?"

"Because I said so."

"We'll see." I laughed and then held up my hand in a small wave. "Good night, Antonio." I turned around and walked toward my building without looking back. I wanted to look back to see the expression on his face, but I remembered how he'd dismissed me at his party and didn't want to give him the satisfaction that he never gave me. As I let myself into the building, I couldn't stop myself from smiling. My life had finally started getting interesting. Antonio was unlike any man I'd ever known in my life, and even though he lived a life that scared me, I knew I wanted to get to know him better.

CHAPTER 25

Antonio

"Revenge is often like biting a dog because the dog bit you." — Austin O'Malley

My eyes watched her until she walked into the building. I was surprised that she didn't look back to see if I was still watching her. Or to give me a final wave. This wasn't how I wanted the night to end. I'd had plans to be in her bed, fucking her to Kingdom Come until she begged me to climax. But the car ride had changed my mind. She was a thoughtful girl. Yes, she was caught up in love the way most women were, but she analyzed and thought deeply about everything around her, including me. I'd nearly slipped up when I'd mentioned that Vee was dramatic. And when I'd said her full name: Callie Rowney. I was only meant to know her first name. That was all she'd told me. Thankfully she hadn't noticed my slipup. I could still taste her against my lips. She'd kissed me back passionately. I hadn't expected that.

I was about to get back into my car when I changed my mind and walked toward the building. I needed to get one last look into her eyes before I went home. My phone beeped as I headed to the entrance.

"Speak," I grunted into the phone as I stared at the keypad at the door. I had no idea what the code was.

"Antonio?" My brother's drawl sounded surprised.

"You called my phone, so yes."

"I just thought I'd get your voicemail. I figured you'd be balls deep inside of her already."

"Slow burn, Alessandro. You can't rush these things."

"The way she was staring at you." He chuckled. "She's into you."

"She doesn't know what she's thinking." I pressed some buttons into the keypad and it flashed red.

"She wants you." He sounded pleased. "She likes you; she doesn't want to, but she does."

"She likes who she thinks I am." The thought displeased me. She didn't know the real me. She didn't know my innermost thoughts. She'd hate me.

She thought I was a good man with a troubled past. I knew better. There was no lightness in me.

"That's good, no?"

"It's great." I growled as I tried another number and the light flashed red. "Let me call you back," I said and hung up the phone before calling Valentina's number. It rang four times before she answered. "What's the code?" I barked into the phone.

"Antonio?" She sounded confused.

"The code for the dorm door. What is it?"

"Why?"

"The code."

"832589," she said quickly. "What's going on?"

I entered the numbers into the keypad and grunted when it flashed green and the door beeped. I pushed it open and stepped inside. It had been a long time since I'd been in a university setting. "What's your room number?"

"Antonio, you're not still bothering Cassie, are you?"

"It's Callie," I said automatically.

"I thought you just wanted to get her to the party."

"What happens next is none of your business." I looked around and walked down a dark corridor. "The room number?"

"We're on the eighth floor. Room J." She sighed. "But you can't—"

"Thanks." I hung up and looked around for the

elevator. I needed to see Callie one more time tonight. I wanted one last kiss. I entered the elevator, feeling tense. I knew I should just go home, but I didn't want to leave just yet. I got off on the eighth floor and looked around. A light sound of laughter made me freeze. It was Callie. I frowned and followed the sound until I rounded a corner. She was standing there, talking to a blond guy in a cap who was leaning against the wall. He had his hand on her shoulder, and I found my hand moving to my gun as I stayed back.

"I was thinking we could watch a movie," he said, staring into her eyes and rubbing her shoulder.

"It's midnight, though…" She looked at her watch and yawned.

"We could do something else." He took another step toward her, and my jaw clenched. "Maybe I could…" His voice trailed off, and I couldn't hear what he said, but I could see Callie blushing. Was this the idiot that had taken her to Central Park with a loaf of bread?

"I should go to bed, Josh." She shook her head, and I watched as her curls cascaded down her back.

"Do you want to have a shower together?" he asked, grinning widely. "I bet the showers are empty." Was this guy fucking joking? Did he think he could flirt with my girl and get away with it?

"I have to go to bed." She took a step back. "Night, Josh."

"Maybe we can talk tomorrow?" he asked hopefully, and she nodded.

"Sure," she said before she headed into a room and closed the door behind her.

"I don't think so," I muttered under my breath as I watched Josh heading toward me. I stepped forward and blocked his way down the corridor, and he looked up at me, frowning.

"Hey," he said, his blue eyes looking confused. "Can I help you?"

"I think so…" I said softly.

"Are you someone's dad?" he asked, and I just stared at him. Was this punk for real?

"I'm Valentina's friend," I said finally.

"Oh." He nodded as if that made sense. "Another one of her fuck buddies."

"Hmm."

"She's not a bad lay." He laughed and held his hand up to high five.

"Is that how you talk about women?" I growled and grabbed him by the shirt. I could see the panic in his eyes as I held him up by the scruff of his neck. "Do I need to teach you how to be a gentleman?"

"Sorry, I was just joking." He paled. "I'm not even into her."

"Oh?"

"Yeah, I have my eyes on her roommate, Callie," he said quickly, and I tightened my grip. "Honest, I do. You can have Valentina." I knew I had to put him down, though my first instinct was to hit him hard.

"The girl I just saw you talking to?" I asked him softly.

"Yeah." He nodded and swallowed hard as I put him down. He took a cautionary step back. "She's a sweet girl. A good girl." He looked over to her door. "I think she could be the one."

"Really?" *In your dreams, buddy.* There was no way I was going to let that happen. I'd have to think of something. I could not have Josh making his move on my little lamb. There was only one wolf that would be feasting on her.

"Yeah." He nodded. "But don't you want to look for Valentina? Shall I go and knock on…"

"I got it." I stared at him for a few seconds. "You stay safe."

"You too." He nodded. "What was your name again?"

I was about to say, "Nonya," like Callie had to me, but I just looked away from him.

"Have a good evening." I leaned back against the wall and rubbed my fingers against the top of my holster. Josh's eyes widened slightly, and I gave him a thin smile. "I think you ought to get to bed now."

"Yes, sir," he said, hurrying away from me. Pussy! I watched to see what room he went into, and then I pulled out my phone.

"Sup, boss?" Jimmy answered the phone on the first ring, like he always did. Jimmy was reliable.

"I need you to do me a favor."

"Oh yeah?" He sounded eager. "Who needs to die?"

"Not who, but what," I said cryptically.

"Tell me more."

"It needs to happen tomorrow." I walked to Callie's door and stood outside, listening for any sounds. I pressed my ear against the door and heard a light giggling. Who the hell was she talking to?

"Boss, you there?"

"Ssh," I hissed into the phone as I tried to listen. I realized I couldn't even call or text Callie as she'd never given me her phone number. I had it, of course, but I wasn't sure how I'd explain having it. I'd have to get it from her when I picked her up in the morning. And then I'd ask to see her phone. Turn on her tracking. Make sure I knew where she was. I heard a scuffling on the other side of the door and ducked back into the corridor and then exited the building.

"You there?" I asked as I made my way back to the car.

"Yeah, boss. What's going on?"

"What do you think about stables?"

"Stables? Like horses?"

"Yeah." I nodded. "I need you to do me a favor for tomorrow."

"Whatever it is. I'm your man."

"I know," I said, a smile crossing my face as I got into my car. Tomorrow would be the day that I lured Callie into my web. Once I had her in my den of deceit, I was never going to let her go.

CHAPTER 26

Callie

"You don't love someone for their looks, or their clothes, or for their fancy car, but because they sing a song only you can hear." — Oscar Wilde

The flowery yellow dress I'd gotten to attend a baby shower last year lay on my bed. Antonio had asked me to wear a dress for the date, but I couldn't imagine that he was thinking of something like this with little graphics of ducks eating sunflowers. I walked over to Valentina's closet and looked at her dresses. She had many cute outfits and one black dress I'd always loved, but I didn't want to be that girl. The one that thought it was okay to borrow her roommate's outfits without asking. And even though Valentina owed me, I would wait until I saw her in person to ask exactly what was going on.

I yawned slightly as I stood there. It was still early, and I was still tired. I grabbed my phone and checked to see if I had any messages. There was one from Josh, and I checked it quickly.

"Valentina's new man was here last night. Be careful. He seems shady."

I frowned slightly at the message. Why was Maksim here without Valentina? Because I was pretty confident she hadn't been back in the room. Was he looking for her? Was she okay? My heart started racing. If Maksim was here looking for her, then that meant she wasn't with him.

"When was he here? Did he say why?" I texted Josh back, but he didn't respond. I had a feeling he was still sleeping. I grabbed my shower stuff and headed to the bathrooms. I needed to get ready. Antonio would be here in twenty minutes for our date, and I didn't want to be late, even though I had misgivings about going. I wondered where he was going to take me. I was excited to see. I only hoped we weren't flying across the country. I'd been serious about that.

~

I hurried out of the building at 7:07 a.m. in a pair of skinny blue jeans and a red-and-white plaid shirt. My hair hung past my shoulders, still wet and curly because I hadn't had time to blow-dry it. My navy-blue sweater was tied around my waist, and my small brown leather handbag contained everything but the kitchen sink.

Antonio was waiting by the door in a pair of black jeans, a white shirt, and aviators, and I could see him tapping his watch as I walked out.

"You're late." He took off his glasses slowly, his brown eyes reprimanding me as I looked up at him.

"It's seven o'clock in the morning." I shook my head. "Give me a break." I yawned again and glared. "You're lucky I even made it up this early."

"You're not wearing a dress."

"I didn't feel like it." I shrugged. "You can't tell me what to wear."

"I asked politely."

"You do nothing politely, Antonio Marchesi."

He grinned then, a wide smile that made his arrogant features softer. His eyes softened as well, and I felt like it was the first time I was really seeing him. The crinkles in the corner of his eyes seemed genuine, and he didn't seem as tense as he normally was.

"Let's start this again," he said softly. "Good morning, Callie."

"Top of the morning to ya, Mr. Marchesi." I gave him a little curtsey, and he burst out laughing.

"You're an idiot, Callie Rowney."

"I am a fair maiden, I'll have you know." I giggled. "Now, where are you taking me on this crazy early date? And does it involve coffee? Because if it doesn't, I'm going to fall asleep on you."

"You're a bossy one in the morning, aren't you?" He sounded surprised. "I thought you might be mad about yesterday still."

"Mad about what?" I asked him as we made our way to his car. My jaw dropped as I saw the black Mercedes GT Coupe sportscar parked on the road. "Is that your car?"

"All four hundred thousand dollars of it." He grinned as he opened the passenger door for me. "Hop in."

"I don't care about your money, you know." I pressed my lips together as he grinned down at me. "That doesn't impress me."

"Never said it did." He slammed the car door shut and ran around to the driver's side. I leaned over and opened the door for him, and he gave me a grateful look as he slid in. "Now, let's get you some coffee."

"Yes, please." I nodded as I put my seatbelt on. "Is this car new?" I asked as I sniffed. It had that new car smell and looked pristine.

"Yes." He turned the keys, and the ignition purred to a roar in the smoothest of ways. "I wanted my first drive in it to be something special."

"Well, we'll see." I laughed, though I was pleased inside. What was my life? I could hardly believe I was here. Imogen would be shocked. Most probably she wouldn't believe me. I was the last person both of us knew that would ever entertain going on a date with a mafia boss, and yet here I was.

"What are you thinking, little lamb?" he asked as he stopped at a light.

"That I can't believe I'm on a date with a mobster."

"I'm not exactly Al Capone." He winked at me. "Or John Gotti."

"Did you ever meet John Gotti?" I asked him, and he chuckled.

"You keep asking me these sorts of questions and I'm going to think that maybe you are with the FBI, after all."

"Yeah, right." I laughed giddily. Being around Antonio made me feel happy. And not just an ordinary happy, but a high happy. It was a floating feeling of pleasure and delight and excitement all rolled into one. Whatever our attraction was, it was dynamic. I felt drawn to him in ways that didn't make sense. "Eek," I screamed as the car suddenly darted forward and we went speeding down the road.

"Hold on, little lamb." He chuckled as he did a quick right turn. I felt like I was a passenger in a car race at the Indy 500 or maybe the Monaco Grand Prix.

"We're in New York City," I gasped. "You can't drive this fast."

"I think I can, and I think I will," he said as he

increased his speed as a light turned amber. I closed my eyes as he sped through the lights. "Don't worry, Callie. I'm not going to kill you in a car crash. That would be too on the nose."

"Huh?" I looked over at him, and he just shook his head as he pulled over.

"Let's get you that coffee and maybe a croissant?"

"Sounds good." I nodded. "Thank you."

"Of course," he said as the car stopped. He grabbed his phone and read something and smiled to himself. I wondered what he was looking at on his screen. Had another woman texted him?

"What's going on with your bride search?" I asked him as he undid his seatbelt. I didn't really want to know, but I wanted to know.

"It's going." He nodded, his eyes moving across my face. "My father has a favorite he'd like me to pick."

"And you're considering it?"

"She's the perfect wife for a mafia underboss." He leaned over and gave me a kiss on the lips. "She knows her place," he whispered gruffly as he sucked on my lower lip. "She knows her duty." His hand moved down the side of my face and lightly grazed against my breast. "In fact, I'm having dinner with her father and family tonight." He slipped his hand up under my shirt, and I gasped as his fingers rubbed against my skin roughly. "Best of all, she wants to be my wife." His fingers slipped into my bra, and I felt them teasing and taunting my nipple. "And I know that she knows how to give good head." His eyes never left mine, and my body arched back as he leaned forward and kissed my neck. I could barely breathe. I was disgusted and turned on at the same time. "Do you know how to give good head, little lamb?" His voice was deep and throaty as his hand moved to my thigh and ran up and down. "Do you think you can fit all eight inches into your mouth?" His fingers parted my legs and ran all the way up. "Will your pussy be able to take all of me?" I felt his palm pressed against my mound, and I could feel a throbbing there. "Do you think about what it will be like to have me inside of you?" His thumb flicked against the top of my jeans, and the button popped open. His index finger deftly slipped the zipper down, and I just sat there, feeling hot and bothered, so turned on that I was unable to speak. "I want to fuck you, Callie," he growled as his fingers slipped down the front of my jeans and rubbed against my panties, trying to move my jeans down so he could have easier access. I bit down on my lower lip. "Are you hoping I choose you to be my wifey, little lamb?" He chuckled slightly, and something inside my brain snapped at his tone.

"In your dreams." I grabbed his hand and pulled it away before quickly pulling up my zipper. My panties felt moist, and I suddenly needed the restroom. "I couldn't care less who you marry, and I certainly don't want to be your wife. In fact, I want to know why you're taking me on a morning date while you're meeting your betrothed for dinner."

He chuckled slightly as he leaned back. "She's not my betrothed, but her father is the consigliere for our family. It would be disrespectful to not attend."

"Because you care so much about being respectful."

"Contrary to what you might believe, I do. We have a very strict code of honor in the mafia." He nodded his head slightly. "And I am a man of honor."

"Yeah, you're so honorable that you were trying to finger-fuck me in your car on our first date before you even bought me a coffee," I spat out, and he laughed.

"That is not true," he said, a wicked smile on his face.

"Uhm, yes, I think it is true," I said, staring at him in shock. "Did you not just undo my jeans and slip your fingers down them?"

"I do not deny that."

"So then you have to admit you were trying to finger me on our first date…" My eyes were on the bulge in his pants that his fingers were resting next to. *Shit, he is packing. Maybe he wasn't exaggerating when he said eight inches, after all.*

"I wasn't trying to finger you, Callie." His voice was hoarse, and his eyes glittered with lust. "I was very much ready to fuck you." He bit down on his lower lip, and he grabbed my hand and placed it on his crotch, moving my fingers back and forth on his hardness. "I'm rock hard, and this is a brand-new car." He chuckled. "I thought we could christen it before we officially started the date. Who doesn't love some morning sex in a brand-new car?" He shifted suddenly, and my fingers dug into his pants. His cock twitched against my hand, and I swallowed hard. I was no longer in the little leagues now. I was in the big leagues, playing with a big boy, and I wasn't sure if I was up for the challenge.

CHAPTER 27

Antonio

"The best revenge is to be unlike him who performed the injury." — Marcus Aurelius

Callie's eyes were on the pastry case in front of her. She was making murmuring sounds as she tried to decide what she wanted to order, and I couldn't stop looking at her. There was something about her that was bewitching. I didn't know what it was, but it was annoying me. Every time I thought I had her under my spell, she'd push back in a way that was unexpected. I shifted uncomfortably as I waited for her to make up her mind. I was hard as fuck. I hadn't intended to touch her when we were in the car, but the way she'd been staring at me and the way her eyes had been begging me for more, I'd not been able to resist. And she'd been enjoying it as well. Her nipples had been hard as pebbles and her panties moist. Her body had also been trembling slightly, and the way she'd kissed me back had been fire.

I frowned slightly as I realized I was staring at her ass. I was an ass man. Well, I was a tits man as well, but I loved a good ass. And Callie looked like she had a plump one. I could just imagine it jiggling when I slapped it and then plunged into her. Fuck, I needed to stop thinking about her fucking her. I hadn't felt this way in a long time. Not since I was sixteen and about to fuck my first woman. And even that feeling had been different. Then I'd been a horny teenager just excited to get laid to a hot nineteen-year-old blonde. Now I was a man, who got laid all the time, yet there was a thrill in the anticipation. I actually wanted to kiss Callie when I fucked her. Which was one of the complaints most women had when I fucked them. I never kissed them, and I never looked in their eyes. I didn't need to. I didn't care about them. But then again, I didn't care about Callie, either. I had to remember that. She was a means to an end.

"I think I'll get the chocolate croissant," she said as she gazed back at me. "And a latte." She looked back to the front. "Actually, maybe I'll get the lemon pound cake." She licked her lips, and I almost groaned out loud. "Actually, maybe the Kouign-amann. It looks delicious." I stepped toward her and placed my hand on the small of her back.

"Why don't you get all of them?"

"I don't need to get all of them." She shook her head quickly. "I can't eat all of them."

"We'll share." I nodded toward the barista and pointed at the pastries. "We'll have one of each, an espresso, and a latte."

"That's too much, Antonio," she hissed, and I laughed.

"It's never too much." I pulled my wallet out and slapped down a hundred dollar note. "Keep the change."

"Thank you, sir." The barista beamed with happiness as she gathered the pastries into a box. Callie was standing there shaking her head and looking displeased, and I wanted to laugh. She really did get upset at the most absurd of things.

"Thank you, sir," Callie whispered under her breath as she rolled her eyes at me, and I laughed.

"I bet she'd fuck me in my brand-new Mercedes on the first date," I whispered in her ear.

"Then go on a date with her, then." She glared at me. "I'm not that sort of girl. I don't go all the way on a first date."

"I don't think you would normally, but you've never dated a man like me before, have you?" I squeezed her ass and then stepped back. "Men like me can make even the good girls turn bad."

"Who said I was a good girl?" she said with a turn of the head, and I felt myself growing hard again as she adjusted her shirt. "You think you know me, Antonio Marchesi, but you have absolutely no idea who I am."

"I don't know about that, little lamb," I whispered back at her, a thin smile on my face. "I think I know exactly who you are."

Callie's stack of books sat in the brown paper bag between her legs, and I smiled to myself. The date had gone perfectly. I'd taken her to a cute little bookstore I knew and told her to find ten books to buy. She'd been shocked but had gone along with it. We'd had a good time. She'd shown me some of her favorite books and acted shocked when I'd said I hadn't read them.

"But this is classic literature," she'd said, shocked, and I'd just laughed. I'd grown up in a world where literature didn't matter, but I didn't want to remind her of that fact. I'd loved watching her pore over books and read through pages excitedly.

"Thank you for the wonderful date." She beamed at me as we pulled up outside her dorm. "I've had a really nice time." She stared at my lips. "It was unexpected."

"What did you expect from me? A drive to my penthouse and a quick fumble in the bed?"

"Well, you did want a fumble in the car beforehand." She gave me a pointed look and I laughed. She was definitely a lot more comfortable around me.

"So you'll go on another date with me?"

"Maybe." She winked, and I stifled a groan.

"You'll come back to work at Lupo's."

"I don't know." She wrinkled her nose. "I hate to say it, but Lucio seems incompetent, and so does Birgette."

"I know," I agreed with her. "I'll fire him."

"What?" Her jaw dropped.

"I want it to be a success." I studied her face. "It is named after me, after all."

"It is?" She stared at me with a questioning look on her face.

"Lupo is wolf in Italian." I ran my fingers through my hair and thought about the name. All these years I moved through the streets as a wolf. A monster to be feared. A beast waiting to bare its fangs, but I actually thought of myself as a different sort of animal. At least, my mom had thought of me as a different animal. Though I never shared that with anyone.

"Oh," she said, her eyes widening. "I didn't know that."

"So yes, the bar has a soft spot in my heart." I touched her arm lightly and smiled warmly. "As do you. I'd love you to continue working there to help me make it a success."

"I don't really have much experience in bars or restaurants," she admitted, blushing slightly.

"But you have heart and brains and ideas." I grabbed her hand and played with her fingers before tracing a circle in her palm. "You can help me make it the place everyone wants to go to."

"I can try." She licked her lips nervously.

"And the date?" I prodded.

"I guess." She giggled girlishly, and I held back a triumphant smile.

"Can I get your phone number?" I asked as I sat back. "Also, I should get you inside before I can no longer stop myself from moving further."

"What do you mean?" She batted her eyelashes at me.

"You're a very beautiful woman, Callie, and I want you very badly. However, I know you're not the sort of woman that just sleeps around, and I don't want to push anything. I respect and care for you too much." I unbuckled my seatbelt and got out of my car before hurrying to open her door. "Let me see you safely to your room. And you can give me your number."

"Okay." She nodded, looking slightly disappointed. A feeling of contentment spread through me. It was just too easy. She stepped out of the car and grabbed her bag of books before I slammed the door shut. We made our way into the building and toward the elevator, and I followed along behind her as if I had no idea where she was going. "I just have a small room. I share it with…"

"Your roommate Vee—Valentina, I remember." I nodded, and she bit down on her lower lip. "What is it?"

"I'm nervous she might not be okay." She sighed. "Josh…a friend of mine, texted me last night and said her boyfriend Maksim was here last night, looking shady, and well, she hasn't been in the room in days, and I thought she was with him, but if he was here in the early hours of the morning, why would he be here?"

I stared at her for a few seconds. I'd fucked up. Josh had texted her. He'd obviously assumed I was Maksim, but I knew if he'd seen me, he'd be able to recognize me. I should have sent him on a trip to the hospital.

"That doesn't sound good," I said, expressing concern. "We should find out what's going on."

"How?" she asked as we walked toward her door. She unlocked in, stepped in, and then I waited. One, two, three. "Arrghhh!" she screamed. "Oh my God, what the fuck…" she cried out as I rushed into the room, and then she screamed again. "Arrrggghhhh."

"What is it, Callie?" I asked her, concerned she was going to faint to the ground. She looked back at me with wide eyes and pointed to a bed in the corner of the room. I pressed my lips together at the side. A bloody horse's head sat on the bed, dead blind eyes staring out vacantly into the room. The white sheets were soaked with a dark-red blood that was also streaked across the floor. "Oh fuck." I grabbed her hand and pulled her toward me. "What the hell? Is this a frat prank?"

"I don't think so," she whispered, her body shaking. "I think someone's taken Valentina. That's her bed."

"It is?" I pursed my lips together. "It's not your bed?"

"No..." She shook her head. "I should call the police."

"Maybe." I nodded and stepped forward to survey the scene. I saw the note on the ground and picked it up. It was dripping with blood, and I read it quickly. I looked back at Callie. "You're not staying here tonight. Whoever left this is a psycho." I held up the note to show her. *"Watch out bitch or you will be next."*

Her jaw dropped as she read the note. "Who would do this?"

"I don't want to scare you, but it looks like the work of a psycho." I held her close to me. "You're staying with me until we figure this out." I could see that she was about to object. "I have spare bedrooms, Callie."

"That's not my worry," she said, shaking her head. "But my dad won't like..."

"He wouldn't want you staying here." I pressed my lips together. "He wants to protect you at all costs. You're his baby girl. His reason for living."

"How did you know that?" she asked, surprised.

"Isn't that how all dads are with their daughters?" My heart thudded, and she nodded.

"Yeah, I guess." She was trembling. "I should text Josh and make sure—"

"Later," I said and grabbed her hands. "Grab some clothes and we'll get out of here. I'll contact the authorities and file a report, so they can clean this up and start investigating," I said in my most authoritative voice.

"Thanks," she said and then let out a low sigh. "I'll stay with you a for a night or two, but that's it." She looked back at the bed and let out a little whimper and closed her eyes. I saw her squeezing her hands together and whispering something under her breath.

"What are you saying?"

"Just singing a song that helps me calm down." Her eyes fluttered open. "Hush, little baby, don't say a word, Mama's going to buy you a mockingbird," she sang in a soft, sweet voice. "My mom used to sing it to me when I was younger." She gave me a sad smile. "It's one of the only memories I have of her. She died when I was young...of cancer."

"I'm sorry." I pulled her into my arms and held her close. "I understand that pain well. My mother died when I was just eight. In a car crash. I never got over her death." I kissed her on top of the head. "I miss her every single day."

"I'm sorry, Antonio." She wrapped her arms around me, and we stood there hugging for what felt like hours before she finally pulled away and looked up at me. "Maybe we really did meet for a reason."

"I told you that," I said with a small smile.

"Maybe we can help heal each other."

"I'm almost positive that you're the only one that can alleviate much of the pain I feel," I said with a small nod. Her brown eyes looked up at me trustingly, soft, innocent, and open, and I felt a sudden stillness. She was pure. Too pure. I'd break her. I'd break her into a million pieces. All of a sudden that possibility didn't give me the thrill I thought it would.

CHAPTER 28

Callie

"To be fully seen by somebody, then, and be loved anyhow —this is a human offering that can border on miraculous."
— Elizabeth Gilbert

My entire body was trembling as Antonio drove me to his apartment. I couldn't get the image of the horse's head out of my mind. All that blood. It was gruesome. A part of me hoped it was just a sick joke, but I had no idea who would do such a thing. I was really worried about Valentina now. Who had left her that threatening note?

My phone started ringing, and I lifted it out of my bag.

"Who is it?" Antonio asked me as he drove at a normal pace. I was glad he was speeding down the road now. My heart wouldn't have been able to take it.

"My best friend Imogen." I was about to send her to voicemail when Antonio spoke again.

"Aren't you going to answer that?"

"Uhm, I was going to wait…"

"Why? Scared to talk to her in front of me?"

"No, why would I be?" I rolled my eyes and answered the phone. "Hi, Imogen."

"Hey, doll, what are you doing?"

"Driving…well, I'm in the passenger seat."

"Ooh, where are you going?"

"To Antonio's house," I said, trying to keep my voice as low as possible.

"Who the hell is Antonio?" Imogen sounded shocked. But then again, she would be. She was my best friend and knew I didn't just go back to men's houses.

"This guy I met the other night," I tried whispering, and Antonio chuckled.

"I have amazing hearing, Callie. Don't try and hide anything from me."

"I'm not." I could hear Imogen's breathing in my ear.

"Was that him?" She sounded excited. "He sounds hot."

"He's okay," I said, giggling, and I froze as I felt his hand on my knee. "But can I call you back? Is everything okay?"

"Girl, why are you going to this man's house?"

"You won't believe me if I tell you."

"What happened?"

"There was a dead horse's head on Valentina's bed."

"Your weird roommate?"

"Yeah." I licked my lips nervously. "I think she's gotten herself into some sort of trouble. Antonio's going to contact the police so they can investigate, but he thinks it's not safe for me to stay in the dorm room right now."

"He thinks?" She sounded suspicious. "Girl, why aren't you staying at your dad's?"

"I don't want him to know." I sighed. "You know he'll make me come home for good."

"So you're staying with this random man."

"He's not random," I protested, even though he really was. I didn't really know what to say to convince her I was being smart.

"You've got the hots for him, haven't you?"

"What?"

"Callie, have you slept with him?"

"It's not raining right now." I looked out the window. "It's quite a nice afternoon."

"What?" She sounded confused. "What are you talking about, Callie?"

"Not nice enough for Coney Island..." I mumbled. "Do you remember that time your dad took us and we got lost and—"

"Callie," she screeched. "I asked you if you slept with him, not about our childhood."

"Imogen," I said slowly, feeling myself blushing. "I think we're going to grab something to eat. I'll call you back." I hung up the phone quickly, and I could hear Antonio chuckling. I looked over at him, and he was staring at me, a teasing look in his eyes.

"You could have just told her, not yet, but soon," he said, smirking, and I hit him on the shoulder. "Keep it up, I like it," he said with a wink, and I withdrew my hand, which made him start laughing harder.

"If you think I'm coming back with you to your place so we can have sex, you're dreadfully mistaken."

"It's a good thing I don't think that, then," he responded smoothly, and I wondered if he was telling the truth. Maybe he was. He hadn't even made a big move on me at the end of our first date. He'd been a perfect gentleman, driving me home and walking me to my dorm room to make sure I made it in safely. He hadn't even hinted at trying to stay over. Not that I thought Antonio Marchesi would ever be caught dead spending the night in a dorm room. Even I wouldn't want our first time to be in my single bed. Not that there was going to be a first time. *Who are you kidding, Callie?* a little voice inside of me poked fun of me. *Antonio would be the perfect first lover. You find him hot. He's caring. He says he wants to get to know you on a deeper level. You know he knows what he's doing. And he feels a connection with you. You might even be able to convince him to leave the mafia world if you fall in love.* I bit down on my lower lip and reached over to turn on the radio to keep the voice in my head from convincing me to strip naked right then and there.

"Where are we going?" I asked suddenly as the car moved onto the highway.

"My home."

"I thought you lived in the city?"

"I have a place in the city." He nodded. "But we're going to the manor. Where we first met."

Coldness covered my face. "Why?"

"I have a dinner date, remember?"

"You're still going?"

"It's not like I'm going to fuck her, Callie. It's just a dinner. It would be a sign of disrespect for me not to show up."

"And I'm meant to go as well? What are they going to say when I show up?"

"I wasn't expecting you to go to the actual dinner." He blinked at me.

"So what? I'm just meant to hide in the bedroom waiting for you? Eating dry bread and moldy cheese?"

"I think we can find some non-dry bread," he joked, but I wasn't smiling. Was he crazy? How did he think this was okay?

"Pull over," I screeched, trying to open the door. On the highway. Maybe I was the crazy one.

"What?" He sounded irritated as he glanced over at me. "What the hell are you doing, Callie?"

"I'm not going to your country estate to sit in some dark room while you have dinner with some woman you're going to marry and her family." I was pissed. "What did you think was going to happen after the dinner, Antonio? You'd come up and fuck me and then go and share a bed with her?"

He let out a deep sigh. "I don't want her. I've already told you that."

I pressed my lips together in silence. My heart was racing, and I was close to tears. He was a hottie, but he was insensitive and rude. I might not have had much experience in life, but I didn't put up with shit.

I pulled out my phone again and called Gia.

"Hey, Callie, how's it going?" She answered the phone quickly.

"Not bad, I'm just—"

"Who are you talking to?" Antonio growled, and I felt his fingers on my arm.

"My friend."

"What friend?" he spat out distastefully. "Josh?"

"No." I pushed his hand away and continued talking. "Are you able to pick me up?"

"Where are you?" she asked me in hushed tones. "Sorry if I'm talking low. I'm in the library."

"I'm in a car, going eighty miles per hour, and—"

"Is everything okay?" She sounded worried.

"Well, An—" I felt the phone being pulled away from my ear. "Hey!" I shouted at Antonio. "What the hell?" My jaw dropped as he rolled down the window and pretended like he was going to throw it onto the ground. "What are you doing?"

"Who are you talking to, little lamb?"

"Gia!" I shouted. "I met her at your party. I was standing with her. I don't know if you remember her?" If he didn't, then something was up because Gia spoke as if she knew him and his brother well.

"I know her." He closed the window again and powered off the phone. "I didn't know you were friends." He pushed my phone in his pocket.

"We just met at the party and bonded." I rolled my eyes. "Turns out she's not a huge fan of the Marchesi men, either."

"Hmph." He shook his head. "Did she say why?"

"No," I admitted. "Give me back my phone."

"Not now." He shook his head.

"You can't just keep my phone, Antonio."

"I don't want you talking to Josh."

"What? Why?"

"I think he might be responsible for the horse's head." He tapped his fingers against the steering wheel rapidly, beating in time to a track in his head.

"What? No way. Why?"

"Didn't he and Valentina used to have a thing? I

think they slept together. He became obsessed with her."

"He did?" I tried to think of all of my interactions with Josh. I knew he and Valentina had hooked up, but neither one of them had seemed that into the other.

"That's why he kept trying to get with you," he continued in a hiss. "He wanted you to get him into the room, so he could be closer to Valentina. Don't you see? Just last night he was waiting for you to get closer to her, but you turned him down. So he finally lost it."

My heart started thudding at his words, a buzz ringing in my ears. I gripped the armrest and tried to regulate my breathing.

"How do you know that?" I murmured, my brain spinning in circles. I hadn't told him about last night and Josh waiting around to flirt with me. And then I realized that I'd never told him about Josh and Valentina, either.

"What do you mean?" he snapped as the car pulled off at an exit.

"How do you know Josh was waiting to talk to me last night and that he and Valentina hooked up and—"

"From my investigator." He sounded annoyed. "How else would I know?"

"I don't know, but how do they know?"

"They spoke to some guys at the dorm already.

My man, Jimmy, is on the case and he texted me."

"I didn't see you getting any texts," I said, frowning.

"They arrived when you were on the phone with Imogen." He sighed. "Do you not trust me, Callie?" He sounded resigned and sad. "I understand if you don't. We don't know each other well, and I guess you just want to think the worst about me, but I'm a good guy."

"I'm sorry," I said quickly. "I just didn't understand how you knew, but I guess if the guys spoke to your friend, Jimmy…" My voice trailed off.

"We can call him now if you want." He grabbed his phone. "You can ask him the names of the guys he spoke to and what they said." He dropped the phone in my lap. "I can give you my code to unlock my phone."

"No, it's fine," I said, twisting in my seat. "I trust you, Antonio. This thing has just gotten me a little rattled."

"I understand." His voice softened as he grabbed the phone back from me. "But I'm here. I will protect you. I'll look after you. I will not let anyone else do anything bad to you."

"Thank you."

"And you can come to dinner as well."

"What?"

"You're right. It's not fair to you that we are dating and I'm going on a dinner without you. You will come to dinner. We will have to find you an appropriate dress to wear, of course, but maybe Elisabetta has some dresses you can borrow."

"Who?" I frowned. Was that his ex?

"My father's housekeeper's daughter," he explained. "Luisa goes with my father everywhere, so her daughter has clothes at all of his houses."

"Oh okay." I nodded. "Was she at the party?"

"No." He shook his head. "She's away at boarding school. Plus she wouldn't be an appropriate wife."

"Why is that?"

"She's the housekeeper's daughter," he said dismissively. "And like my little sister. I watched her grow up." He snorted. "And she has an unbearable attitude." He looked over at me. "A bit like yours, actually."

"Thanks for the compliment."

"You're welcome." He chuckled. "So now, are you feeling a bit better? You'll dress up and come to dinner, and the next few days you will stay with me so I can make sure you're safe."

"I'm feeling fine." I nodded. "Can I get my phone back? I will need to call my dad."

"You'll tell him where you are?" He sounded surprised.

"Not exactly," I admitted. My dad would blow a gasket if he knew I was spending the next few nights with a hot, older mafia boss. He'd think I'd lost my mind or become a woman of the night or something. I giggled at the thought. My dad was always so extra.

"What's so funny?" Antonio asked. I could hear the frustration in his voice, and it made me smirk. He didn't like not being in the know.

"Nothing. I was just thinking about some of the things my dad might say if he knew where I was."

"He wouldn't be happy?"

"I mean, would you be happy if your daughter was dating a mob boss…" I paused. "Well, I guess you wouldn't care."

He smirked and didn't respond. I watched as he pulled his phone and made a call. "Papa? It's me, Antonio. Tell Tommasso we need to change the dinner to tomorrow night." He looked over at me and gave me a warm look. "I have something to take care of tonight. I don't care." His voice sounded deadly. "I'll be at the manor in fifteen minutes. I have a guest. Tomorrow at seven. I have nothing else to say." He hung up and smiled at me. "Tonight you have me all to yourself."

"You didn't have to change the plans." I shook my head. "I don't care."

"You had a fright today, Callie. I just want to hold you in my arms and comfort you." He reached out and touched my hand. "Like I said earlier, your well-being is my concern. I've never experienced something like this before. I want to…see where it goes."

My heart raced at the sincerity in his eyes. He

looked like he was close to crying. I could see myself falling for this man. If I was honest with myself, I already was. I felt like I was a princess in a fairytale and I was about to get my happily ever after after all. Maybe the stories were true. Maybe the fair maiden really could tame the dark, tormented monster. Maybe the wolf didn't eat the lamb, after all. Instead maybe they just cuddled in his den and kept warm together.

"You will get your own room, of course." He spoke softly. "I do not want to make you feel uncomfortable."

"Thank you, Antonio." I squeezed his hand. "But tonight I think I'd like to sleep in your bed."

CHAPTER 29

Antonio

"I waited all my life for revenge and yet it didn't taste as sweet as I'd hoped." — Antonio Marchesi

It shouldn't have been so easy. It almost felt too easy. An emotion akin to regret filled me as we walked along the dark corridor toward my bedroom. Callie's warm hand was in mine, and I could feel her heart racing through her palm.

"You really didn't have to change the dinner to tomorrow night," she said as I stopped outside of my room. I pushed her back against the door and held her there for a few seconds before speaking.

"You might not have been in my life for a long time, but I want to make you feel comfortable. I want to show you I'm not the man you think I am."

"And what sort of man is that?" she whispered up at me.

"The sort of man that doesn't care about how you feel."

"You care about how I feel?" Her brown eyes spoke of her pleasure as she gazed at me. "The man that chased me from his party cares about me?"

"I more than care about you." I pressed my lips into her neck and ran my fingers down her arms. "You're the sort of woman that can make a man forget his own name." The words sounded fake even to my own ears, but the dull ache in my heart told me that they weren't completely false. I was getting too close to Callie. She was too trusting. Too sweet. Too eager to believe in what I had to say. She desperately wanted love. She believed in happily ever afters.

"Let me see your room." She reached up and touched my lips, and I felt my entire body stiffening at the way her eyes lit up in mischief. "Or should I say your wolf den?"

"I call it my mole habitat," I whispered without meaning to. I already regretted telling her something so personal.

"What?" She sounded surprised. "Why do you call it that?"

"No reason, it was a joke, better than saying come into my lair, little lamb, I want to gobble you up."

"Maybe I want you to gobble me up." She licked her lips. "Maybe I want to be a bad girl tonight."

"Oh yeah?" I asked her, my heart pounding with lust. I wanted Callie very badly.

"Can I ask you a question, Antonio?"

"Anything."

"What were the ropes for in your car?"

"Not what you think." I laughed, grabbing her hands and pulling her into my room. I switched on the light and closed the door. I watched her looking around with wide eyes at my large, king-size bed and walnut furnishings.

"What are they for?"

"Have you heard of Shibari?" I asked her, guiding her toward the bed. The time for talking was done. I had other needs that needed to be met.

"Nope." She shook her head. "What is that? A dog? Are you buying me a puppy?"

"What?" I threw my head back in laughter. Only Callie could make me laugh like this. Not even Alessandro.

"Oh wait, that's Shiba." She grinned. "I got confused for a few seconds."

"I'm not getting you a puppy." I pushed her down on the mattress gently. "Unless you want one, of course."

"I can't have pets in the dorm." She wrinkled her nose.

"I can keep it at my penthouse, if you want." The

words were out before I could think about what I was saying. I hated pets. And dogs especially. There was no way I wanted a puppy in my house, getting in the way.

"You'd do that for me?" Her eyes lit up, and she reached up and pulled me toward her. Her lips pressed into mine, and I growled against her mouth as her tongue worked its way into mine. Her fingers squeezed my shoulders, and I ran my own to her breasts, brushing over them wantonly, needing to touch and feel her.

"I'd do anything for you." I gasped as her fingers ran idly down my thigh toward my crotch. I pushed her onto her back and yanked her top off. I was hot and hard. The little dance of foreplay between us had gone on too long. I was done playing games. I was ready to take what was mine. And Callie Rowney was mine. Every single atom. She lay on her back, staring up at me with wide eyes, and my lips fell to her stomach, kissing up her body toward her breasts. She ran her fingers through my hair and let out a squeal as my mouth clamped down on her nipple through her bra. I arched my back as I lifted her up slightly and pulled off her bra and threw it to the ground.

"You're not playing." She giggled slightly as my mouth fell to her naked breast and took her puckered nipple into my mouth. She tasted hot and salty, and teeth sank into her breasts gently as my fingers played with her other breast. Her entire body purred at my touch, and for a moment I forgot I was a beast and monster. I kissed up the valley between her breasts and licked up her neck to her mouth.

"I'm going to devour you, Callie." My voice was hoarse as her fingernails ran down my back. "I'm going to fuck you so hard and so deep that you're going to realize that every man that's come before me is a mere mortal."

"And you're what?" She gasped as my hand slid down to unzip her jeans.

"I'm a sex god." I slipped my fingers into her pants and rubbed between her legs. I grinned in a self-satisfied way when I felt how wet she already was. No lube would be needed with Callie. I grew even harder thinking about how easily my cock would glide inside of her. Fuck, I needed to be inside of her now. I was growing a temperature just thinking about her pussy walls closing in on me. She'd definitely be a screamer. That I could tell already. I debated locking the bedroom door. The last thing I needed was my dad or Luisa walking in on us fucking. I didn't care, but I knew Callie would be self-conscious.

But then she pushed me back and moved to take my shirt off, and I knew I wasn't getting off the bed to do shit. She was more aggressive than I'd thought she'd be in bed. Which delighted me. I was glad she was one with her sexual being. It would make this all the more fun. I didn't want a timid woman that was scared to speak up or please me.

"So what's Shibari?" she asked me as my top came off and her lips pressed against my abdomen. I looked down into her wild face; her lips were puckered, and her eyes were gleaming.

"It's a Japanese word that means binding or tying, and in this context, between us, it means bondage."

"Bondage?" She paused, her eyes wide.

"Yes, my dear. I will tie you up with ropes and give you the best sex of your life." I pushed her back onto the bed and pulled her jeans off. "But not tonight. Tonight I will just fuck the living daylights out of you." I stared at her panties and licked my lips as I pulled them off. I was surprised to see that her womanhood was half-shaved in an odd fashion. "What's this?" I asked her, staring at her pussy in confusion.

"I attempted to give myself a Brazilian." She made a face. "It didn't work."

"You attempted it yourself?" I raised an eyebrow, and as she blushed, I started laughing.

"It's not funny," she said in an embarrassed tone.

"It's hilarious." I shook my head, just staring at her naked body. She really was one in a million.

"Do you not want to go down on me now?" She looked away from me, and I reached my fingers between her legs and rubbed her clit gently.

"Why would you think that?" I muttered in a

hoarse tone as she spread her legs and looked up at me with desire in her eyes. I leaned down to kiss her, and she melted against me. I slipped a finger inside of her, and she cried out slightly. Her body was shaking, and I loved it. My thumb grazed her as I slipped a second finger inside of her.

"Oh my gosh..." she cried out, and I kissed back down her body, not leaving a spare expanse of skin alone. I picked up her right leg and licked all the way down to her ankle before massaging her foot. Then I sucked on all of her toes and grunted as I saw her gripping the sheets tightly. My tongue licked all the way back up her inner thigh, and then I parted her legs all the way before diving in.

She cried out as I slipped my tongue inside of her, my fingers on both sides of her torso. She tasted as sweet as honey, and I knew I would never get enough of her. I let the tip of my tongue flick back and forth against her clit before diving back inside of her.

"Antonio," she screamed, her heads pulling my hair as her body buckled up and down. She exploded in an orgasm, and I licked her clean, loving the way she was moving and screaming. "Oh my gosh, that was amazing," she gasped as I kissed back up her body. I went to kiss her, and she moved her mouth away. I frowned down at her.

"You don't like to kiss during sex?" I felt strangely

annoyed. That was my thing, but I was making an exception for her.

"It's not that," she said, shaking her head and going bright red.

"Then what?"

"Your lips are still wet." She pressed her lips together, and I growled as I got it.

"You've never tasted your own sweetness?" I laughed as I grabbed her head and kissed her passionately. My hand on the back of her neck as my tongue licked around hers. She moaned slightly and then kissed me back even more passionately. She had really only been with boys. My fingers played with her breasts before unbuckling my own pants and pulling them off. I was harder than I could ever remember being. I needed her. I jumped off the bed to pull my boxers off, and she stared as I held my cock in my hands.

"Like what you see?" I whispered as I got back on the bed. She nodded and reached out and touched me lightly. My cock twitched in response, and she giggled. I frowned slightly as I looked at her. "Is there a problem?"

"Yeah." She nodded looking serious. "I think I'm not interested in you." She wrinkled her nose. "I think I should go."

"What?" My jaw dropped as I stared at her naked body. Fuck.

"I'm just joking." She threw her head back and laughed. "Got you."

"Oh, hell no." I grabbed her hands and held them above her head, my right hand holding her wrists together tightly as she wiggled on the bed beneath me. "You think it's a good idea to play around with Antonio Marchesi?"

"Why not?" She winked at me. "Is the wolf going to punish me for being a naughty girl?" she teased me, and I felt something in me melting. My left hand trailed down her body softly, enjoying every gasp she made and every twitch of her muscles. If I wasn't careful, I was going to start enjoying this far more than I should. I tensed and hovered above her body, letting my cock graze across her stomach.

"Is that going to fit?" She swallowed hard as her fingers ran up and down my shaft, squeezing gingerly. She ran her finger back and forth across the head and squeezed, and I almost blew my load then. Never before had a woman gotten me this hard, just from a touch.

"I guess we'll have to see." I chuckled as I spread her legs. I positioned my cock at her opening and rubbed it back and forth against her clit, wetting her again for my entrance. I didn't bother asking her about protection. From what Valentina said, all the college girls were very sexually active and on the pill. And I knew I was clean. I got tested every sixty days, and I hadn't had intercourse in a couple of months.

Even though I'd had many offers, I'd had other things on my mind.

"Antonio," she gasped as she tried to free her arms. "I…I'm…" She moaned as I rubbed my cock against her entrance.

"Yes, little lamb?" I leaned down and kissed her lips as I inched my way into her wet pussy. If she'd never been with a man as big as me before, then I didn't want to hurt her. As soon as the thought hit my brain, I froze. I wasn't a man to take mercy. I arched my back and moved to thrust into her deep and hard. She wanted this. She could take it. I'd fuck her so hard, she wouldn't be able to walk tomorrow. And she'd beg me to do it again. I let go of her wrists and grabbed her hips and pulled her down slightly. The tip of my cock eased inside of her, and I made a move when suddenly she reached up and touched the side of my chest.

"I'm a virgin," she gasped, her eyes nervous, and I froze.

"What?" I stared at her trembling lips, the scared and excited look on her face, and I cursed under my breath.

"I want to do this, though," she said quickly.

"You wait until I'm almost knee-deep inside of you before you tell me you've never been fucked before?" I jumped off of the bed, my cock standing to attention, feeling cold as I paced back and forth.

"Antonio." She jumped off of the bed and touched

the side of my back, her breasts pressing into my arm. "I want you to be my first. You've already been my first real orgasm."

"But all your dates? The other men...or rather the boys?"

"We never went very far." She sounded embarrassed. "I wanted it to be with someone special, that I knew would—"

"Someone special?" I turned to her and grabbed her face. I stared down into her eyes.

"Well, I mean, it's not like I was specifically waiting for a mafia boss or anything." She rolled her eyes. "That wasn't on my top ten list of wants. One, handsome; two, kind; three, sexy; four, a mafia boss." She jutted out her chin and her lips twitched slightly. I felt my anger seething slightly. I wasn't really sure who I was angrier at, her or myself. I pulled her into me.

"It's going to hurt."

"I know that." She rolled her eyes.

"I mean it will hurt more than normal." I nodded down toward my cock. "I'm larger than average."

"I agree, your ego is humongous." She giggled, and I picked her up and carried her back over to the bed and laid her down.

"You think you can get away with that?" I growled as I traced the silhouette of her body. She was beautiful.

"Get away with what?" She licked her lips. "Are you going to tie me up now?"

"You wish," I grunted as I hovered over her again. My fingers reached down again to make sure she was still wet. I needn't have worried. She was even wetter than before. "Fuck, Callie."

"Yes, please," she moaned as she pulled me down to her. "Fuck me, Antonio. It's okay. I want this."

"What would your dad say?" I looked into her eyes, searching.

"He'd be pissed." She giggled. "Maybe he'd want to kill both of us."

"Good." I bit down on her lower lip and started to inch myself into her. "I'll be as gentle as possible. It might hurt at first, but I'll try not to completely ruin you."

"Do your best." She whimpered and arched her back into me. Her breasts pressed against my chest, and I knew I was about to lose control. My cock slid inside of her as slowly as possible. Her pussy walls clung to me, never wanting to let me go, as her fingers dug into my skin. Her breathing was harsh underneath me, and I knew I couldn't hold back much longer. I lifted her legs slightly and thrust into her a little faster. I felt her wall trying to stop my invasion and then thrust into her a little harder. She cried out, but I kept going, inch by inch, until I was almost completely inside of her. I paused and looked down into her face. Her lips were parted, and she was delirious. I kissed her hard and then moved in and out of her, ensuring my thrusts weren't too hard and fast.

"Oh fuck, Antonio," she whimpered in my ear.

"Say my name." I grew harder inside of her at her words.

"Antonio, fuck me, please, harder."

She didn't have to say the words again. I increased my pace, burying my cock so deep inside of her that I was worried I'd disrupt her internal organs. She was so tight and so wet and her very essence seemed to be invading all of my senses as I took her on the wildest ride of her life. I reached down and rubbed her clit as I slid back and forth, our bodies becoming one as her breathing grew even more intense. And then I felt her body shaking as she reached orgasm, and I thrust into her hard and fast, closing my eyes as I felt my own orgasm coming. She clung onto me as I dove into her. Then my body froze for a few seconds before I exploded inside of her, filling her with my cum, loving the feeling of her pussy being filled with my seed. I pulled out of her slowly and looked down. My cock was covered with her blood. And it pleased me knowing no other man had had her. No other man had been inside of her. And now she was completely mine. I kissed her on the lips, and she touched the side of my face.

"Wow." She grinned at me. "Maybe you're not so bad after all."

"You think?" I said as I pulled her into me. "How was it?"

"Amazing." She licked her lips. "I've never felt anything like that before."

"I know." I laughed as I ran my fingers across her stomach. "We'll have to get you on the pill."

She looked up at me, a wide-eyed expression on her face. "Oh shit, I forgot about that. My mind was focused on other things."

"Don't worry." I kissed her. "We can get you the morning-after pill."

"Okay." She smiled as she touched my shoulder. "How was it for you?"

"Mind blowing," I admitted honestly. "I wish you weren't a virgin, though."

"Why?"

"Because I'm ready to go again." I chuckled as I played with her breasts. "But I don't want to overdo it for your first time."

"I want to," she said, running her fingers down my chest. She shifted slightly and then gasped.

"What is it?"

"The sheets." She looked down below as they were soaked in blood. "I'm so sorry. I didn't know."

"Don't apologize." I laughed. "But maybe we should enjoy a shower first."

"First?"

"Before we go again."

"Oh, okay." She smiled and nodded. "Together?"

"Is there another way?" I grabbed her hand and pulled her up. "Come, let's go." I led her toward the bathroom, already hard again. We walked inside, and I stared at our reflection. She looked well loved, with wild, crazy hair, a beautiful womanly body, with large breasts and a plump ass. She stood there with a wicked, anticipatory smile on her face. And then I looked at myself. My dark hair was messed up. Light stubble grew on my jawline. My body was hard, muscular, the same as it always was on the outside, but something inside of me felt different. I pulled her into my arms and pressed her up against the bathroom door hard, my erection pressing against her stomach.

"You're driving me crazy, Callie."

"Oh?" She ran her hands down to my ass and squeezed. "I thought you were crazy before we first met."

"Maybe." I laughed before I stepped back. I turned the water on in the shower and waited for it to become warm before grabbing her hand and pulling her into the large standalone shower. I grabbed a bar of soap and ran it over every inch of her body, loving the way her silky skin felt. Then I ran the soap downward and lathered it up into a foam before grabbing my razor. She stared at me with wide eyes, and I laughed as I started to shave her. "Don't worry, I'll go slowly," I said as the machine glided back and forth on her skin, dark hairs falling to the ground and going down the drain. She stood there playing with my hair, and when she was finally shaved clean, I dropped to my knees under the cascading water and lifted one of her legs over my shoulder before burying my head in her pussy and eating her out. She cried out as my tongue flicked and licked, and I was gratified when she came again quickly.

I then stood up and grabbed her and hoisted her up, pushing her back into the wall as she wrapped her legs around my waist. I thrust into her deep, hard, and fast, and she screamed as she bit down into my shoulder. I fucked her hard and fast, her breasts bouncing as her back went back and forth against the wall. I had a carnal need to fill. I paused as I shifted her ass against the wall and then continued fucking her. I let her down gently before bending her in front of me. My fingers played with her puckered asshole, and she shifted slightly. I laughed as I thrust back inside of her pussy and moaned as she cried out, her hands against the glass in front of her.

"Oh yes, Antonio!" she screamed. "Yes, yes." I continued making her mine, erupting into her in an explosion of epicness as she screamed one last time. Before I knew what was happening, the door to the bathroom was open, and Jimmy was inside.

"Boss…" he asked, a gun cocked in his hand ready

to shoot. "Oh…" He grinned lasciviously as he took in Callie's naked body and processed what was going on. "Sorry, I thought there was a problem."

"No problem," I grunted. "Get out of here, Jimmy."

"Yes, boss." He licked his lips, and I could feel anger welling in me as Jimmy stared at her breasts.

"Out." My voice was hoarse, and he nodded and left.

"Sorry." I pulled Callie around to look at me. "I should have locked the door."

"Not your fault," she murmured, leaning up to kiss me. "I guess I was a bit loud."

"Just a bit." I laughed, wrapping my arms around her waist. "I shouldn't have fucked you so hard just now. You're going to be sore tomorrow."

"I'll be fine," she said, shaking her head at me.

"Trust me, doll. You're going to have a hard time walking," I said as I pressed my manhood against her. "And every time you take a seat tomorrow, you're going to remember me deep inside of you, making you mine."

She swallowed hard as she looked up at me, and I could see her blushing. I loved the fact that she didn't try to mask her emotions.

"And then when the sun starts to set, you'll get excited and wet just thinking…" My voice trailed off as she gave me a puzzled look.

"Thinking about what?"

"How many hours you have left until you can have my dick again." I chuckled as I bit down on her lower lip. "There will come a time, little lamb, when all you'll be able to think about is the next time you can have me inside of you." I traced my fingers down her slender neck and grinned.

"What if that time is now?" she said, grabbing my cock, a wicked grin on her face, and it was my turn to gasp. Maybe my little lamb wasn't so shy after all.

CHAPTER 30

Callie

"I waited all my life for love and yet it didn't taste as sweet as I'd hoped." — Callie Rowney

Antonio had not been joking when he'd said I was going to be sore. I could barely walk, and my thighs felt sore. Let alone everything else. It was a weird feeling, but not one I hated. Making love had been even more fantastic than I'd imagined it being. And I knew the first few times weren't even meant to be that good. I couldn't wait to see how much better it got. I couldn't even begin to imagine it. I smiled to myself as I sat on the couch in Antonio's private living room reading a first edition of *Pride and Prejudice* that Antonio had gotten me from the library to read.

He'd had to do some work and had left me in his

suite of the house while he had explained to the police what we'd found in my dorm. I tried not to think of the horse's head. It just made me queasy, and I was so grateful that he'd offered to take care of it for me.

The more I got to know Antonio, the more he surprised me. He was a really compassionate man. Even if sometimes he had a dark look in his eyes, like he was far away. I also tried to ignore the Spidey sense in my head that said something wasn't adding up. Everything was almost too perfect. He was saying too many of the right words. The way he talked, he was close to falling in love with me, but I'd read and watched many books and movies. The hard, cold bastard never turned that quickly. But then life wasn't like the movies, and he'd never met anyone like me before. I refused to believe that what I was feeling wasn't real. Our attraction and chemistry were like magic. It was amazing. I leaned back and grabbed my phone. I had several missed calls and texts from Imogen, Gia, my dad, and Josh. I scrolled through the texts quickly. Imogen and Gia were checking up on me to see where I was and if I was okay. My dad was apologizing again for not being a better provider and saying he was going to do better. I was going to have to talk to him. I couldn't continue with his coddling. I loved him, but he hadn't lived his life for years. And I didn't want him to die never knowing love again. I was confident my mother wouldn't have wanted that.

I was about to call my dad when another text came through from Josh.

"**Hey Callie, where are you?**"

"**Hey,**" I responded. "**I'm at a friend's place.**"

"**Are you okay?**"

"**Yeah, I'm fine.**" He must have seen the police carrying out the horse's head. I was glad I hadn't been there.

"**When will you be back?**"

"**Not sure yet. I guess when the police say it's okay.**"

"**The police?**"

"**Oh, didn't you see them when they came to remove...the head?**"

"**The head?**"

"**The horse's head.**"

"**Callie? What are you talking about?**"

Maybe he'd been out when they'd cleaned up the scene. Though I was surprised everyone on the floor wasn't talking about it.

"**Oh, just something in Valentina's and my room.**"

"**Talking of Valentina. I saw her and her boyfriend Maksim yesterday.**"

"**Oh good, so she's okay?**"

"**Yeah...she's fine.**"

"Yay!" I let out a deep breath. At least I didn't have to worry about her anymore.

"**But the guy I saw...he wasn't Maksim.**"

"Huh?"

"**Remember I told you about that man I saw... the one that tried to intimidate me?**"

"**Oh yeah...what do you mean it wasn't Maksim?**"

"**The guy I saw with Valentina this morning wasn't the same guy.**"

"**Oh weird. Who was it, then?**"

"**I don't know. But I have a weird feeling. You sure you're okay?**"

"**I'm fine, Josh. I'll text you later, okay? Need to call my dad.**"

"**Okay...talk soon.**"

I was about to put my phone down when he texted one more time. "**You can stay in my room, if you need to.**"

I ignored his final text. Was this all a big ruse to get me into his bed? Did Josh think I was an idiot? I couldn't believe I'd even given him a shot. He was a boy in comparison to Antonio. I shook my head and decided to call my dad.

"Callie, darling? Where are you?"

"Just getting ready for class, Dad," I lied and then exhaled. "Dad, we need to talk. I think that..." My voice trailed off. I didn't know how to tell my dad he needed to let go.

"I agree," he said with a sigh. "There are some things I need to tell you." He sounded resigned, and my heart thudded with worry.

"Are you okay, Dad?" I said in a panicked tone.

"I'm fine. I spoke to a friend of mine that still works at the mayor's office. There's something I need to tell you."

"Oh?"

"It's about your mother's death…" He sounded sad. "It was my fault."

"How was it your fault, Dad? She died of cancer."

"Yes, but I wasn't a good husband."

"Dad, you were a great husband."

"I wasn't," he protested. "I cheated on your mom, Callie. I will never forgive myself. In fact, on the day that she died, I was with…" His voice cracked, and I felt my body growing cold. He wasn't lying. Was this why my father had given up his life? Out of guilt, rather than heartbreak?

"Dad, what are you saying?" My voice was cold, and then I heard the door opening. Antonio stood there, a quizzical look on his face as he stared at me. My heart raced as I stared at him. I was so grateful to have Antonio in my life. I needed him. "Dad, I will call you back. I have to go." I stood up, dropped my phone onto the couch, and then walked over to Antonio and hugged him. He pulled me in close and rubbed my back.

"Is everything okay?" he whispered against my hair.

"Yes." I pressed my lips against his neck. I didn't want to talk about any of it. "Is it nearly time for dinner?"

"Yes," he said, pulling away from me. "You're sure you want to do this?"

"Yes." I nodded. "I don't want that Serena thinking she has a chance." I grabbed his hand, and he chuckled.

"My dad will be there." His eyes were dark as he looked over my face. "He's not a nice man."

"I can hold my own," I said, trying to sound confident. His dad had looked like a mean, controlling troll when I'd seen him at the party. "He doesn't intimidate me."

"Good." He nodded. "Because if you think I'm a monster, then you've never met him."

"Hey, last night, you mentioned you were more like a mole than a wolf," I said, remembering his words suddenly. "What did you mean by that?"

He stared at me for a few seconds wordlessly. His face was almost stoic, and he looked slightly pained. He shook his head as if he wasn't going to answer.

"You can trust me, Antonio," I said softly as I gazed up at him with love in my eyes. "With anything." He looked thoughtful for a few moments and nodded.

"Wolves are pack animals. They travel together.

They begin mating when they are two to three years old, and then they establish lifelong mates." He grunted. "That's not who I am. Moles are solitary animals that rarely leave their tunnels unless by accident. They create extensive burrows in search of their prey, but they are antisocial creatures. That is me. I like to be alone. I like my space. I don't need or want people." He shrugged. "When I was growing up, I always liked my own space. My mother named me her little mole. She told me that she understood what it was to need your own space."

"Oh wow." I wondered if he was still a mole. Did he still want to be alone? Or would he allow me into his space?

"And when she died, the only person that truly knew and understood all of me was gone." His voice cracked. "And I vowed on that day, at her funeral, that I would have one goal in life: to make those who were responsible for her death pay."

"That sounds ominous." My heart fluttered in fear. There was a veil of a threat in his voice, and I didn't understand why.

"Not really." He chuckled and grabbed my hand. "Let us go. It is time to eat."

"Okay." I nodded, brushing my hair back as we exited the room. We headed down the dark corridor, and it seemed that it was never-ending. "Is this the right way?" I asked, blinking in the increasing darkness.

"Yes," he said, his voice hoarse.

A loud wail cried out suddenly, and I froze. "What was that?" My breathing was coming fast now.

"A bat." He chuckled. "They live in the other wing in the house. There's an attic that runs across that wing. Sometimes you can hear the wailing."

"Creepy." I grabbed his hand. "Don't walk so fast."

"Don't worry, Callie. I'm here." His voice comforted me as he squeezed my hand. "Hold on a second," he said as he stopped suddenly. He reached down and handed me a bronze candelabra with a white candle and lit it. "I forgot something in the room. Stay here. I'll be right back."

"Can't I come with you?" I frowned.

"I'll be right back." He left before I could say anything else. I stared down at the flame moving back and forth, barely lighting up the corridor. I stood there, trying to ignore the anxious thoughts starting to fill my brain. I stared at the candelabra and blinked. It looked familiar. Was I having deja-vu? Where had I seen this before? And then I gasped. It was the same candelabra from my dreams. How was that possible?

I heard footsteps coming toward me, and I froze. Was that Antonio? Was he back already? The hushed tones of talking alerted me to the fact that it was someone else.

"Elisabetta wants to go to Italia..." an older lady's

voice stated. "She will need money."

"I do not think that is a good idea," the deep, gruff voice answered. It sounded familiar. And then they turned the corner and were right next to me. It was Antonio's dad, Roberto. The don himself. I knew I'd recognized the voice. An older lady in a maid's outfit stood next to him, and I was pretty sure she was the housekeeper Antonio had told me about.

"Phillippa…" The man's eyes almost bulged out of his face, and my heart stopped. How did he know my mother's name?

"It cannot be?" The older lady stepped forward. "Phillippa?"

"No…" My voice trembled, and I was about to scream when I felt Don Roberto's hand on my dress, pressing back hard. His fingers smelled of tobacco, and I wanted to throw up.

"Do not be scared." His dark eyes surveyed me as he looked me up and down, his grubby finger suddenly in my hair as he smiled. I could feel my body trembling with fear as they both stared at me. My knees buckled, and I suddenly fell to the ground, the candle flame singeing my skin as it fell on me. Don Roberto got on his knees and touched the side of my face.

"It's okay." There was a cackle in his voice. "Hush little baby, don't say a word, Momma's gonna buy you a mockingbird.," he sang in a cracked, deep voice, and I felt faint. He was singing my mom's song. How did he know? What the hell was going on here? And then came the wail again, this time louder and more insistent, and he pulled away from me.

"Luisa, go upstairs now," he growled, a menace in his voice that made me shiver. Where the hell was Antonio? Like magic, I heard his footsteps coming back down the corridor.

"Little lamb, where are you?" he called in the darkness.

"She's here," Don Roberto said, glee in his voice as he stood up, taking the candle with him. "When were you going to tell me?"

"Tell you what?" Antonio sounded pissed as he reached his father. "What have you done?"

"When were you going to tell me you had Philippa's daughter?" his face contorted as his mouth hissed. "Or are you going to tell me you didn't know?"

"I am Antonio 'The Wolf' Marchesi," Antonio's voice boomed down the corridor. "I know everything." And with that, my head sank back and blackness took over, the voices inside screaming at me for being such an idiot. I had no idea what was happening, but I knew I was in trouble. How did these two men know my mother? And what did that mean in regard to the last couple of weeks of my life?

Thank you for reading Of Monsters, Men, & Moles The final book will be out in April. You can check out a bonus chapter here.

About the Author

If you enjoyed this book and would like to connect with Natalia Lamb, here are her socials.

Facebook Page

Private Facebook Group

Instagram

Tiktok

Join my Natalia Lamb mailing list.